Lantry dragged her to him, encircling her with his strong arms....

Her lips parted, opening for him, and she felt the tip of his tongue sweep over her lower lip. It had been so long since she'd felt desire, felt it run like a fire through her veins, felt it blaze across her skin.

She would have been shocked had she thought about how badly she wanted this man, but at the moment all reason had left her. Her body ached with a need for this cowboy and Dede threw all caution to the wind as he swept her up and carried her to the loft.

B.J. DANIELS

ONE HOT FORTY-FIVE

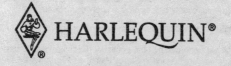

HARLEQUIN®

TORONTO • NEW YORK • LONDON
AMSTERDAM • PARIS • SYDNEY • HAMBURG
STOCKHOLM • ATHENS • TOKYO • MILAN • MADRID
PRAGUE • WARSAW • BUDAPEST • AUCKLAND

This one is for Danni Hill and her wonderful bookstore, Promises. Thanks for letting me be a part of it.

Recycling programs for this product may not exist in your area.

ISBN-13: 978-0-373-69428-0

ONE HOT FORTY-FIVE

Copyright © 2009 by Barbara Heinlein

www.eHarlequin.com

Printed in U.S.A.

ABOUT THE AUTHOR

B.J. Daniels wrote her first book after a career as an award-winning newspaper journalist and author of thirty-seven published short stories. That first book, *Odd Man Out,* received a four and a half–star review from *Romantic Times BOOKreviews* magazine and went on to be nominated for Best Intrigue for that year. Since then she has won numerous awards including a career achievement award for romantic suspense and many nominations and awards for best book.

Daniels lives in Montana with her husband, Parker, and two springer spaniels, Spot and Jem. When she isn't writing, she snowboards, camps, boats and plays tennis. Daniels is a member of Mystery Writers of America, Sisters in Crime, International Thriller Writers, Kiss of Death and Romance Writers of America.

To contact her, write to B.J. Daniels, P.O. Box 1173, Malta, MT 59538 or e-mail her at bjdaniels@mtintouch.net. Check out her Web site at www.bjdaniels.com.

Books by B.J. Daniels

HARLEQUIN INTRIGUE
 996—SECRET OF DEADMAN'S COULEE†
1002—THE NEW DEPUTY IN TOWN†
1024—THE MYSTERY MAN OF WHITEHORSE†
1030—CLASSIFIED CHRISTMAS†
1053—MATCHMAKING WITH A MISSION†
1059—SECOND CHANCE COWBOY†
1083—MONTANA ROYALTY†
1125—SHOTGUN BRIDE*
1131—HUNTING DOWN THE HORSEMAN*
1137—BIG SKY DYNASTY*
1155—SMOKIN' SIX-SHOOTER*
1161—ONE HOT FORTY-FIVE*

†Whitehorse, Montana
*Whitehorse, Montana: The Corbetts

CAST OF CHARACTERS

Lantry Corbett—The divorce lawyer was about to learn what happens when one of his client's wives shows up with a gun.

Dede Chamberlain—There was more to this angelic, blue-eyed beauty than met the eye.

Frank Chamberlain—He'd been anything but the perfect husband.

Shane Corbett—The sheriff's deputy was trying his best to keep his brother out of jail and out of the clutches of a deadly divorcée.

Violet Evans—The local woman escaped from the mental hospital. Now nothing could stop her from getting revenge on the people of Whitehorse.

Arlene Evans—She feared her dream wedding with Hank Monroe would never happen.

Ed Ingram—He knew all about family bonds— and what happened if you betrayed them.

Tamara Fallon—Her jewels had been stolen and she'd disappeared. But was there more to the story?

Chapter One

Every nerve in Dede Chamberlain's body was tense as she lay on the narrow bed in the barred, locked room. She listened to the late-night sounds: weeping, an occasional scream, the scrape of a chair leg at the nurses' station down the hall.

Dede knew better than to fall asleep. She'd heard that a new orderly had been hired, and she knew what that meant. She hadn't seen him yet, but she'd heard about him through the whispers of the other patients. A big guy with light gray eyes and a scar on his left cheek. Claude.

She didn't know his last name, doubted he would have used his real one for this job anyway. But she knew Claude would come for her tonight now that only minimal staff were on duty.

But there was no chance of escaping this place. After she'd escaped from the Texas facility, they hadn't taken any chances with her up here in Montana. They'd put her in the criminally insane ward under maximum security, assuring her she couldn't get out—and no one could get to her.

And they thought *she* was the one who was crazy?

The men after her *would* get to her. There was no escaping them—not while she was locked up.

The air around her seemed to change. She sensed it, the same way she had sensed her life coming unraveled just months before. No one had believed her then; no one believed her now.

Dede leaned up on one elbow, the metallic taste of fear in her mouth, a taste she'd become intimately familiar with since she'd discovered just how far her husband would go.

Battling back the fear, she vowed she wouldn't make it easy for Claude when he came to kill her. It was all she had left—she would give him one hell of a fight.

From down the hall, she heard a door open and close with the careful stealth of those who lived by secrets and lies. Dede sat all the way up, listening to the cautious squeak of shoe soles as someone crept down the hallway in her direction.

Another door opened with a soft click; another pair of shoe soles sneaked down the hallway.

Furtively Dede rose from the bed and padded to the door to peek out through the bars into the dimly lit hallway.

Two figures moved as quietly as cockroaches. She recognized them as patients and started to turn away. Whatever they were up to, she wanted no part of it.

But then one of them saw her.

From down the hall, Violet Evans shot her a warning look and touched her finger to her lips before dragging it dramatically across her throat.

Dede had seen her the day she'd been captured and

brought in. Violet had watched her through the bars of her window. After spending the last month in a psych ward, Dede recognized madness. But when she'd met Violet's gaze that day, she'd known that she'd just seen true insanity.

"Who is that woman?" Dede had asked the armed orderly taking her to her room.

"Violet Evans. We all watch out for that one."

Violet was a raw-boned woman, late thirties, with straight brown hair and a plain face. The other patient beside her now in the hallway was a large buxom woman with a visage like a bulldog. Both seemed to be carrying what looked like a bright red blanket over one arm—only Violet had one over each arm.

As Violet motioned to someone down the hall at the nurses' station on the other side of the steel bars, Dede felt her stomach roil. She'd heard that Violet had tried to escape from here once before and it had gone badly. She was sure it would be worse tonight and wanted no part of it.

Dede started to step back as Violet came alongside her door. But before she could move, Violet stepped in front of the barred, open window. For the first time, Dede was glad that she was locked in.

She touched her finger to her lips to let Violet know she'd gotten the message loud and clear and wasn't about to give them away. Anyone with a brain could see that the woman was dangerous.

Violet nodded slowly, and Dede saw what she was carrying. Not a blanket. Two plush Santa Claus suits. Dede frowned. Were the costumes from the Christmas program she'd heard about that patients on the other side of the hospital were practicing for? But how did Violet—

The sudden blare of the fire alarm made Dede jump.

But it was the closer, quieter sound that sent her heart racing: the soft clunk of her cell door unlocking.

Through the bars of her window, Dede saw Violet smile and mouth, "You're coming with us."

The door swung up, and Violet reached in, grabbed her by the wrist and dragged her out into the hallway. Violet shoved a Santa costume at her before giving her a shove toward the confusion at the end of the hallway.

"Come on, Texas escape artist," Violet said. "Let's see if you can get out of *here* alive."

LANTRY CORBETT WASN'T USED TO the phone ringing in the wee hours of morning. Unlike his brother Shane, who was a deputy sheriff, Lantry's business didn't require middle-of-the-night calls.

That's why it took him a few minutes to realize what had awakened him.

"Yeah?" he said after fumbling around half-asleep and finally snatching up his cell phone.

"Lantry?" Shane's voice made him reach for the lamp beside the bed. The light came on, momentarily blinding him. His bedside clock read 3:22 a.m. His pulse took off, and he sat up, scaring himself fully awake.

"Sorry to call you so late, but one of your clients has been arrested and is demanding to see you."

"What?" He threw his legs over the side of the bed and dropped his head to his free hand. "You scared the

hell out of me. I thought something had happened to…" He shook his head as he tried to shake off the fear that this call was about their father.

It had been a crazy thought, since the family had turned in early down at the ranch's main lodge, and none of them would have been out on a night like this.

Lantry padded barefoot to look out the front window of his cabin toward the main ranch house a good quarter mile away. Nothing moved, no lights shone, no sign of life. Everyone was in bed asleep—but him and his brother Shane.

Snow covered everything in sight, and more was falling, making the night glow with a white radiance. For a moment, he stared at the snowflakes suspended in the ranch yard light outside, wondering what he was still doing in Montana.

"Lantry, are you listening to me?"

He hadn't been. "There's some mistake. No client of mine is in your jail cell. All my former clients are in Texas." Which was where he should be—and would be, once Christmas was over.

"Not this one. She has the Texas accent to prove it," Shane said. "Look, this is kind of a special case, or I wouldn't have called you at this hour. They're coming for her at first light to take her back."

"Back to Texas?"

"Back to the state mental hospital here first, then back to the mental facility she escaped from in Texas."

Lantry let out a curse. "A *mental patient?* Why would you believe her when she said she was my client?"

"She asked for you by name."

He shook his head, still half-asleep he assumed, since this wasn't making any sense. "Who is this woman?"

"Dede Chamberlain."

Lantry let out a string of curses. "The woman's *crazy*. Why do you think she's been locked up? You call me in the middle of the night for this?" He started to hang up.

"She says it's a matter of life and death—yours. She swears your life is in danger because you were involved in her divorce."

Lantry couldn't believe this. "I represented her *husband* in the divorce. I've never even laid eyes on this woman, and I can't imagine why *I* would be in danger. Frank Chamberlain was extremely happy with the job I did for him." Lantry thought of how well paid he'd been. "The only danger I might be in is from his lunatic ex-wife. Just keep her locked up until the hospital comes to take her back."

"She said you might need convincing. If you refused to see her, she said to tell you to have someone check the brake line on your wrecked Ferrari."

"My wrecked *Ferrari?*"

"I know, you don't have a Ferrari," Shane said.

No, but he *had* owned a Lamborghini. That was, until the accident just before he'd left Texas. His stomach lurched at the memory of losing control of the car. He'd been lucky to get out alive.

"I'll call her a court-appointed attorney," Shane was saying. "Sorry to have woken you for nothing. But she was so convincing, I felt I had to call."

"What time did you say they were coming to get her?"

JUST BEFORE FIVE O'CLOCK, Lantry walked into the Whitehorse, Montana, sheriff's department brushing snow from his coat. "Is Dede Chamberlain still here?"

Shane looked up in obvious surprise to see him standing in his office doorway. "Yes, but I didn't think you were interested in representing her. Something change your mind?"

"Can I see her or not?" Lantry asked.

"You might want to work on your bedside manner."

"I'm a divorce lawyer, not a doctor, and after being rudely awakened, I couldn't get back to sleep."

Shane picked up a large set of keys. "I had forgotten you get a little testy when you don't get your rest."

Lantry didn't take the bait as he followed his brother through the offices toward the attached jail. He nodded to a deputy who didn't look like he was out of high school, obviously a very recent hire given the fact that his uniform looked straight out of the box.

Shane led Lantry through a door and down a hallway between a half-dozen cells. All but one was empty. He noticed that Dede Chamberlain had been put in the last cell at the end of the row and guessed that was probably because she'd been disruptive and they hadn't wanted to hear it.

Lantry had dealt with his share of young wives married to rich older men. He knew the type. Privileged, spoiled, demanding, born with a sense of entitlement.

As he neared the former Mrs. Frank Chamberlain's cell, he saw a small curled-up ball under what looked like red fake fur. He cleared his throat, and she sat up looking sleepy-eyed for an instant before she became alert.

Lantry had never laid eyes on the woman before and was more than a little surprised. Dede Chamberlain had already been locked up in the Texas mental facility by that time so the only person Lantry had dealt with was her lawyer. When he'd handled her husband's side of the divorce, he'd assumed the fiftyish Frank Chamberlain hadn't been far off base when he'd claimed his younger wife was a gold-digging, vindictive, crazy bitch who was trying to take all of his money—if not his life.

Having seen his share of crazed trophy wives, Lantry had put Dede Chamberlain in the same category. He'd expected Botoxed, health-clubbed and hard as her designer salon acrylic nails.

That's why he was taken aback now. This woman looked nothing like the ex-wives he'd dealt with during his career.

Dede Chamberlain had the face of an angel, big blue eyes and a curly cap of reddish-blond hair that actually looked like her original color. There was a sweet fresh-ness and innocence about her that he'd always asso-ciated with women from states that grew corn.

But if anyone knew that looks could be deceiving, it was a divorce lawyer.

She blinked at him as if surprised to see him, then rose to come to the bars. "Thank you so much for coming down here, Mr. Corbett," she said in a voice that was soft, hopeful and edged with maybe a little fear.

"I'm not here to represent you."

"You're not?" She lost the hopeful look.

"If you weren't already locked up and facing life in

prison or worse, I would have you arrested for whatever you did to my *Lamborghini.*" He stopped and frowned. "Why are you wearing a Santa Claus costume?"

She waved a hand through the air. No acrylic salon fingernails. Not even any polish on her neatly trimmed bare nails, he thought, distracted for a moment.

"The Santa suit? It's a long story," Dede said. "But you probably shouldn't hear about it since you aren't my lawyer. But for the record, I never touched your car. You can blame Frank for that."

Lantry shook his head. "Why would your ex-husband and *my* client, who I might add I got a huge settlement for, want to destroy my car?"

"I can understand your confusion, Mr. Corbett. But that's why I had your brother call you. Your life is in danger because of something my ex-husband was involved in."

Lantry nodded, wishing he hadn't bothered to come down here. What had been the point? The woman had escaped from a mental institution. Two mental facilities, actually, and had shown a history of fanatical behavior on the verge of homicidal during the divorce. Had he expected reason from this woman?

He shook his head and turned to leave.

"Why do you think I'm in Whitehorse if not to warn you?" she said to his retreating back. "Why come all the way to Montana? Why not just take off to some place where no one could find me and save my own neck? Isn't that what you would have done?"

That stung, but he couldn't deny the truth of it. He stopped walking away and turned to look back at her, something in her words making him hesitate.

"I would be dead right now if it hadn't been for the two inmates who broke me out with them from the state hospital," Dede said.

"Instead, you came here to *save* my life."

She nodded, obviously missing the sarcasm in his tone—or ignoring it. "My motives weren't completely altruistic," she said. "I'm hoping you can save us both. But if they—"

He held up his hand to stop her. "Who's *they?*" he asked, waiting for her to say she didn't know so he could walk out without feeling the least bit guilty. "I thought you said *Frank* was behind this death wish for me?"

"Actually, it's two childhood friends of Frank's," she said. "I only know them as Ed and Claude. But when they showed up in Houston, that's when Frank began to change. I could tell he was afraid of them, but it was as if they had some kind of hold on him."

This all sounded like a bad B movie, and Dede Chamberlain was writing it from somewhere inside her demented brain.

Lantry had heard his share of pre-divorce stories over the years. He didn't want to hear Dede Chamberlain's, didn't want to feel any sympathy for her. Marriage was a choice, and she'd stupidly married Frank.

Those big blue eyes filled with tears. She bit her lower lip as if fighting to hold them back. "I know those men are why Frank turned on me—and why they're now trying to kill you."

He couldn't help but ask. "Didn't you question him about what was going on?"

"He said I was imagining things. But one night

after he'd had a few drinks, he seemed to be the old Frank I'd fallen in love with. He said that he'd believed a man could change, could overcome his past, even his upbringing. I said I believed that too, but he said we were both wrong. That his past had come back to drag him down, and there was no escaping it."

"What does any of this have to do with him trying to kill you or me?" Lantry asked impatiently.

"Didn't you ever ask yourself why it wasn't enough for Frank to just divorce me? He had me committed so no one would believe anything I said."

And it was working, Lantry thought.

"Last week Frank called me and warned me they would try to kill me and that I had to get out of the hospital."

Lantry rubbed the back of his neck. His head hurt, and he needed sleep. "You do realize how crazy this all sounds, don't you?"

She nodded. "They're counting on you not believing me. That's why you have to get me out of here so—"

Lantry let out a laugh. "I don't think so. I'll take my chances with Frank and his boys. But thanks."

"They tried to kill you once when they rigged your Ferrari," she said grabbing the bars of her cell, calling after him as he started to turn away again.

"*Lamborghini*," he said, turning back to her.

"Whatever. All those kinds of cars look alike to me," she said and glanced at her watch. "We don't have much time, Mr. Corbett. I'm your last hope. Once they kill me, there won't be anyone who can save you."

Why was he still listening to this woman? Because

of an uneasy feeling that her story was just crazy enough to be true.

"How did you get to Montana anyway?" he demanded, wanting to trap her in a lie so he could wash his hands of this whole business and get back to bed. "Frank took all the money, the cars, the houses—"

"I have my own money, Mr. Corbett." There was a hard edge to her voice. "I didn't marry Frank for his, no matter what he led you to believe."

Lantry couldn't hide his surprise. He had wanted to believe she was a crazy gold digger. It made what Frank did to her easier to be a part of. "Even if I believed that Frank's buddies tampered with my car, they had other chances to kill me after that. So why haven't they tried?"

"I suspect they didn't know where to find you," she said. "Ed has got to be in Whitehorse by now. Claude is either still at the hospital or on his way here. If I have to go back in the mental hospital, he'll kill me. He came close in Texas. I'd be dead right now if Violet and Roberta hadn't broken me out. I know all this is hard for you to believe—"

The cell-block door opened, and his brother stuck his head in, motioning to him.

"Hold that thought," Lantry said to Dede, shaking his head at how foolish he was to buy into any of this. So the woman had her own money and she was no dummy, her story was still preposterous.

"We just got a call," Shane said. "A stolen vehicle believed driven by one of the patients Dede Chamberlain escaped with has been spotted. The patient, Violet

Evans, is from here. The sheriff and I are going out there now. Are you about through with your client?"

"She's not my client," Lantry snapped irritably. His cell phone rang. He checked it. "I need to take this."

"Deputy Conners will be here in case you get any ideas about breaking her out," Shane joked.

Lantry mugged a face at his brother and took the call as the cell-block door clanged shut. "So, what did you find out?"

"How about 'Hello, James, sorry to wake you too damned early in the morning and ask you to track down my wrecked car.'"

"Sorry." James Ames was a close friend and a damned good mechanic. "You found it? And?"

"The brake lines weren't cut."

So it was just as he'd suspected. Dede Chamberlain was delusional.

"The steering mechanism was hinky, though."

"Hinky?" He glanced down the line of cells at Dede, then turned his back to her.

"I've never seen one torqued quite like that from an accident," James said. "What did you hit?"

"Nothing. I just suddenly lost control of the car. Are you saying it had been tampered with?" Lantry said, keeping his voice down.

"Only if someone was trying to kill you." James laughed as if he'd made a joke. "I guess in your profession that's always a possibility, though. Guess they missed you this time." He was still chuckling when Lantry hung up.

He glanced back at Dede again. She was holding on to the bars, watching him with that hopeful look on her angelic face again. Damn.

As he walked back to her cell, he pictured Frank Chamberlain, a handsome, well-to-do, powerful man in Houston who didn't need to resort to murder to get what he wanted. "You say Frank called to warn you. But if Frank wanted to protect you, why didn't he break you out himself?"

"How did Frank tell you he made his fortune?" she asked, the change of subject giving him whiplash.

"A killing on Wall Street."

She smiled ruefully. "He told me his grandmother left him the money."

Lantry had never cared how his clients made their money as long as he got paid. Frank Chamberlain had paid right away. The check had gone through, and Lantry had put the case behind him and gone to Montana for a family meeting on the Trails West Ranch, where his father and new wife had just settled. He hadn't planned to stay so long, but he'd gotten involved in some family legal business and then it was almost Christmas....

"Frank lied to both of us, and worse, involved us in his past." Dede met his gaze with a challenging look. "You're starting to believe me, aren't you?"

The woman didn't know a Lamborghini from a Ferrari. Did he really think she knew the brake line from the steering mechanism?

"Even if I bought into this, the state is sending someone to pick you up in—" he glanced at his watch "—less than—"

Her bloodcurdling scream made him jump back. She began to rattle the bars, screaming at the top of her lungs.

"What the hell are you doing?" he demanded and reached out to stop her.

She grabbed the front of his shirt and the strings from his bolo tie. He heard fabric rip as he tried to pull away, the bolo tie tightening around his neck. The door to the sheriff's office clanged open, and the still-wet-behind-the-ears deputy came running toward them.

It all happened so fast. Lantry made the mistake of trying to calm her, afraid he would hurt her if he pulled away too hard. Dede had wound her fingers into the fabric of his shirt and was hanging on to his bolo tie as if it were a lifeline.

The deputy jumped into the middle of the ruckus.

Lantry didn't see her get the deputy's gun. It just suddenly appeared in Dede's hand, pointed at the two of them at the same time the screaming stopped.

In the deafening silence that followed, all Lantry could hear was the blood pounding in his ears as he stared at the woman with the gun.

Dede was so calm now he shuddered to see that she knew her way around weapons and probably the steering mechanisms on Lamborghinis as well. He couldn't believe how he'd been taken in by her. Probably the same way poor Frank Chamberlain had.

The deputy had turned a sickening shade of green.

"Take it easy," Lantry said, not sure if the words were meant for Dede or the deputy or himself. "Don't do anything rash." How could she do anything more rash than what she'd just done short of shooting them both now at point-blank range?

She barked out instructions to the green deputy, who did as he was told. "Now put the plastic cuffs on the lawyer. Loop them through that fancy belt of his."

"Like hell," Lantry said.

"I'm sure you don't want to see anyone get hurt here, do you, Mr. Corbett?"

He glared at her.

She pointed the deputy's pistol at the young man's heart. "Make sure they are good and tight."

Lantry had no option. He couldn't take the chance she would shoot the deputy.

"Now open the cell," she said, still holding the gun on the deputy. "Hurry up. We don't want to see any innocent people get hurt because you didn't move fast enough."

As instructed, the deputy opened the cell and traded places with her. Dede closed the cell door, keeping the pistol on Lantry, and took the keys.

"Come on, Mr. Corbett. We'll be leaving now. Cross your fingers that no one tries to stop us. As crazy as I am, who knows what I might do?"

Lantry bit down on a reply and, with the gun barrel pressed into his back, let her lead him out of the sheriff's department and into the snowy, still-dark early morning.

Chapter Two

There were no cars in the parking lot other than Lantry's pickup and the deputy's beat-up old Mazda, both covered with snow. The blizzard Lantry had been warned about on the news had finally blown in.

"Just a minute." Dede reached into his coat pocket and dug out his cell phone and keys. She hit the automatic lock release, the lights of the pickup flashing on.

As Dede walked him to his pickup, wind whirled the large, thick flakes around them as if they were in a snow globe.

He could imagine how ridiculous the two of them looked. Him in handcuffs tethered to his belt and a petite woman in a Santa costume holding a gun on him.

But unfortunately, there wasn't anyone around at this hour—and in the middle of a blizzard—to see them.

"You don't want to do this," Lantry said as they reached his pickup. "This is only making your situation worse."

"A hotshot lawyer like you? I'm sure you can get me off without even any jail time," Dede said, keeping the pistol pressed into his back.

"You can't possibly think that I can make all of this go away. You pulled a gun on a sheriff's deputy and escaped from two mental hospitals and a jail cell."

"I did what I had to do," she said, pressing the gun barrel into his back. "When the time comes, I know you can make a judge understand that. Anyway, what would you have done under the same circumstances?"

He didn't know. He thought of his brother Dalton's criminally insane first wife. The law didn't always protect people. Oftentimes it was used against the person who needed and deserved protection the most.

Dede took him around to the driver's side and opened the door. "Get in and slide across the seat. If you think about doing anything stupid, just think about your part in helping Frank take everything—including my freedom from me—in the divorce."

He climbed in and slid across the seat, keeping what she had said in mind. He had helped put this woman away—just not well enough, apparently.

She followed, never taking the gun off him and leaving him little doubt that she really might shoot him if he tried to escape.

Shifting the weapon to her left hand, she inserted the key and started the pickup, then hit the child locks and reached over to buckle him in. "Just in case you're thinking about jumping out."

As if he could reach the door handle the way she had him hog-tied.

The wipers swept away the accumulated snow on the windshield. The glow of Christmas lights on the houses blurred through the falling snow, a surreal reminder that Christmas was just days away.

Dede turned on the heater, then shifted the truck into gear and, resting the pistol on the seat next to her thigh, drove away from the sheriff's department.

Her composure unraveled him more than even the gun against her thigh. This woman must have nerves of steel. For just a moment, though, he thought he saw her hands trembling on the wheel, but he must have imagined it given the composed, unwavering way she had acted back in the jail.

They passed only one vehicle on the way out of town. A van with a state emblem on the side, but the driver was too busy trying to see through the falling and blowing snow to pay them any mind.

Lantry consoled himself that the deputy would soon be found in the cell and a manhunt would begin for the escaped prisoner and her hostage.

"You'll never get away with this," he said, his throat dry as she took one of the narrow back roads as if she knew where she was going.

He recalled that she'd spent the past twenty-four hours before her arrest with Violet Evans, a woman from the area. It was more than possible that Dede had gotten directions from the local woman.

"I suppose all this seems a little desperate to a man like you," she said quietly.

"A *little* desperate?" He looked over at her, then out at the storm. He could feel the temperature dropping.

The weatherman had forecasted below-zero temperatures and blizzard conditions. Residents had been warned to stay off the roads because of blowing and drifting snow and diminishing visibility.

Lantry had little doubt that the roads would be closed soon, as they had been earlier in the month during the last winter-storm warnings.

"You know, it's funny," Dede said as she drove. "Thanks to Frank, I've been forced to do things I wouldn't have even imagined just months ago. I suppose that *is* nuts, huh?"

Lantry studied her, not wanting to know what had pushed her over the edge. "Would you have really shot that deputy?"

"Of course not. What do you think I am? That deputy never did anything to me. Unlike you," she added. "You helped Frank get me locked up in a mental ward."

Lantry didn't want to go down that road. The wind rocked the pickup. Snow whipped across the road, forcing Dede to slow almost to a crawl before the visibility cleared enough that she could see the road ahead again.

The barrow pits had filled in with snow. Only the tops of a few wooden fence posts were still visible above the snowline.

"My brother will be combing the countryside searching for me," he said. Outside the pickup window he could see nothing but white. There were no other tracks in the road now. No one would be out on a night like this. *No one with a brain,* he amended silently.

"Shane will call in the FBI since kidnapping is a federal offense," he continued. "This time they'll lock you up and you'll never get out. Do you have any idea where you're headed?"

He glanced over at her when she didn't answer. Her angelic face was set in an expression of concentration and determination.

"The best thing you can do at this point is turn around and go back," he said. "If you turn yourself in, I'll do everything I can to make sure you get a fair hearing."

"I'm touched by your concern, Mr. Corbett. But I'm crazy, remember? *If* I get caught, they'll just put me back in the looney bin and throw away the key, and then the men after me will kill me. By then, they will have murdered you, so you'll be of little help."

She shifted down as a gust of wind rocked the pickup and sent snow swirling around them.

"But if we don't get caught," she continued, "I might be able to keep us both alive. So in the grand scale of things, kidnapping you seems pretty minor, don't you think?"

He hated that her logic made a bizarre kind of sense. She wasn't going to turn around and take him back, that much was a given.

In the rare openings between gusts, blurred Christmas lights could be seen along the eaves of ranch houses. But soon the ranch houses became fewer and farther between, as did the blur of Christmas lights, until there was nothing but white in the darkness ahead.

They were headed south on one of the lesser-used, narrow, unpaved roads. Between them and the Missouri Breaks was nothing but wild country.

"What now?" he asked as the wind blew in the cracks of the pickup cab and sent snow swirling across the road, obliterating everything.

"You're going to help me save our lives—once I convince you how much danger you're in."

It wasn't going to take much to convince him of that, Lantry thought as he noted the gun nestled between her thighs and the Montana blizzard raging outside the pickup.

DEDE GRIPPED THE WHEEL AND fought to see the road ahead. Mostly what she did was aim the pickup between the fence posts—what little of them wasn't buried in snow on the other side of the snow-deep barrow pits.

Between the heavy snowfall and the blowing fallen snow, all she could see was white.

She didn't need Lantry Corbett to tell her how crazy this was. But given the alternative…

Nor did she want to admit that the lawyer's arguments weren't persuasive. There was a time she would have believed everything he said and been ready to turn her life over to him, thinking he would save her.

But this wasn't that time. Too much had happened to her. And too much was at stake. A part of her wished she'd been honest with Lantry back at the jail, although she doubted it would have swayed him anyway.

She couldn't let herself forget who this cowboy was or the part he'd played in bringing them both to this point in their lives.

This Lantry Corbett, though, looked nothing like the man she'd only seen on television. This blue-eyed cowboy hardly resembled the clean-shaven, three-piece designer-suited lawyer who she'd been told would eat his young.

She'd thought she had the wrong Lantry Corbett when she'd rolled over on her cot in jail earlier and had seen the cowboy standing outside her cell. This man wore a black Stetson, his dark hair now curled at the nape of his neck—not the corporate short haircut he'd sported in Texas—and he'd grown a thick black mustache that drooped at the corners and made him look as if he should have been from the Old West.

Maybe even more surprising, he looked at home in his worn Western attire. This was no urban cowboy, and the clothing only made him more appealing, accentuating his broad shoulders and slim hips. Even the way he moved was different. Tall and lanky, Lantry had walked into the jail with a slow, graceful gait in the work-worn cowboy boots and Wrangler jeans that hugged those long legs.

He had been nothing like that ultraexpensive lawyer she'd seen stalking across the commons of his office high-rise with a crowd of reporters after him.

No, for a moment in the jail, she'd been fooled into thinking she was wrong about the cutthroat divorce lawyer turned cowboy—until he opened his mouth.

Only then did she know she had the right man.

She kept her attention on the road—what she could see of it—and the blizzard raging outside the pickup, wishing there was another way.

VIOLET EVANS ALWAYS KNEW SHE'D come home one day. She'd thought about nothing but Whitehorse since she'd been locked up.

True, she had planned to come home vindicated. Or at least have everyone believe she was cured. But that hadn't happened.

In the passenger seat of the stolen SUV, Roberta began to snore loudly.

Violet knew everyone in four counties was looking for her. She'd become famous. Or infamous. Either way, she liked the idea of her name on everyone's lips. They'd all be locking their doors tonight.

She smiled at the thought, imagining the people who'd wronged her over the years. They would be terrified until she was caught. Once, they'd just made fun of her. But now they would have new respect for her.

Still, it bothered her that they all thought something was wrong with her. No wonder they'd been quick to send her away to a mental hospital after that unfortunate incident with her mother. How different things would have been if they had believed her when she'd tried to explain why she'd tried to kill her mother that day.

She shoved away the disturbing images from the past. But one thought lingered. If Arlene loved her... If she'd saved her from her awful grandmother... If she'd tried to help her with the scary thoughts in her head...

A mother is supposed to save you. Arlene Evans had failed to save her oldest daughter, so what right did Arlene have to get married and be happy?

"No right at all," Violet's dead grandmother said from the backseat. "Her idea of saving you had been to marry you off."

Violet thought of the humiliation and embarrassment when no man had wanted her—and worse, the disappointment she'd seen in her mother's face.

"If Arlene hadn't tricked my son Floyd into marrying her and had you three kids—"

"Can you just shut up?" Violet said, wishing she could cover her ears. She'd heard this from her grandmother since she was a girl. Grandmother always causing trouble, stirring things up between them, then standing back and saying, "See? See what I mean about this family?"

Roberta stirred in the passenger seat. "What's going on?" She glanced in the backseat, then at Violet, frowning. "You aren't talking to your dead grandmother again, right?"

"I was talking to myself. I need you to run a little errand for me," Violet told her as she parked near Packys, a convenience store on the edge of town.

She had skirted Whitehorse, which wasn't difficult since the town was only ten blocks square and she knew all the back roads.

The first thing she needed to do, though, was find out everything she could about her mother's upcoming Christmas wedding. It wasn't like she'd gotten an invitation.

"You're going to run in and get me the local newspaper and the shopper—those are the area bibles when it comes to what's going on," Violet told her.

Roberta groaned and complained, but finally got out and went in. She was wearing a pair of blue overalls and a flannel shirt and looked enough like a local that she shouldn't have any trouble, Violet figured.

Getting a change of clothing had been easy since Violet knew which residents would be gone this time of year and which ones locked their doors. They'd tossed out the Santa costumes after tossing out Dede Chamberlain.

It had amused Roberta to dump Dede on the main street of Whitehorse wearing the Santa suit.

When Roberta returned from inside the convenience store with the newspaper and free shopper, Violet drove down the street the few blocks past town. She pulled over in front of Promises bookstore, gift shop and antique store—closed now—and took the papers from Roberta.

Snapping on the dome light, she scanned for what she knew had to be there. Whitehorse, Montana, was so small that weddings, baby and wedding showers, and birthday parties were advertised in the paper and open to everyone. Her grandmother had already said that Arlene would invite the whole town to show off the fact that she'd caught another man.

To her dismay, Violet didn't find anything about the wedding and was about to give up when she saw the wedding shower announcement.

There was no address as to where the shower was being held, since it was unnecessary. Instead all that was listed was the name of the person who was hosting the get-together. Pearl Cavanaugh. If you didn't know where the Cavanaughs lived, then you had no business at the shower.

"What the hell?" Violet said, thinking she must have read it wrong. "Pearl Cavanaugh is throwing a shower this afternoon for my mother? This has to be a misprint."

"I thought you said nobody in town liked your mother."

Violet shot Roberta a look that shut her up. Maybe it was a pity shower. Still, it seemed odd. Violet couldn't shake the uncomfortable feeling that everything had changed since she'd been gone.

She read it again and noticed something she hadn't seen before. It said in case of bad weather, the shower would be held at the Tin Cup, the restaurant out of town on the golf course.

Violet had heard about the winter-storm warning on the radio. She couldn't imagine worse weather.

Her thoughts returned to her mother and the shower. It was amazing enough that her mother had found another man when Violet hadn't even found one. And he was a man with money, from what she'd heard. She consoled herself with the assurance that Hank Monroe couldn't be much of a man.

"So, are we going to your mother's shower?" Roberta asked, reading over her shoulder.

"I wouldn't miss it for the world. But first there's somewhere we have to go."

ARLENE TOUCHED THE WEDDING dress hanging from her closet door.

She felt like Cinderella about to go to the ball. She closed the closet door as the phone rang. All morning she'd feared that Pearl would cancel the shower. After all, with this storm coming in… "Hello?"

"Hi, beautiful."

She melted at the sound of Hank's voice. That she'd been given a second chance was such a blessing. He'd changed her. Not that she didn't have a long way to go.

She still had to bite her tongue not to gossip or have uncharitable thoughts. Hank laughed at her attempts to be the perfect woman.

"Arlene, I love you exactly as you are." That alone amazed her. But she wanted to be better for Hank. His love had already made her a better person.

"I hope I didn't wake you," Hank said now.

"No, I was up admiring my wedding dress." Hank had bought it for her, saying she deserved her dream wedding. She and Floyd, her first husband and the father of her children, had gotten married by the justice of the peace. A shotgun wedding because she'd been pregnant with her first born, Violet.

Looking back, it was clear Floyd had never wanted the children. Nor did he care about them even now. He hadn't even been to see his own grandson.

Arlene was so thankful that Hank loved the baby and had gone out of his way to help her daughter Charlotte and son-in-law, Lucas, make a home for their son.

"Then you haven't seen the news," Hank said, dragging her from her thoughts.

Arlene felt her heart drop. "No, why?" Her first thought was that the shower was cancelled. But from the sound of Hank's voice, she knew it was more serious than that.

Her worry intensified. Instinctively she knew it must have something to do with Bo. In the past, most news, especially bad news, was often about her son, Bo. But Bo was gone.

She still couldn't believe what he'd done to bring about his own death. For months now, she'd mourned his loss, knowing she had failed him by spoiling him, just as she'd failed her daughter Violet by not spoiling her enough.

"Honey, it's Violet. She's escaped from the state institution. There were three of them. One has already been caught, so I'm sure—"

"Ohh." She sat down hard in the middle of the floor, the phone clutched in her hand. *"Violet?"*

Her oldest daughter. The culmination of all her mistakes as a mother. Hank kept assuring her that she hadn't made Violet what she'd become. That there had been something wrong with Violet, something genetic. Just as she couldn't blame herself for the way Bo had turned out after growing up without a father present.

Arlene couldn't help but feel that if she'd been a better mother, if she'd insisted Floyd take more of a part in raising the kids, if she'd been able to stand up to Floyd's horrible mother and not let that old woman near her kids…

"I want you to come stay with me until Violet is caught," Hank was saying.

Caught? How was it possible to raise a child that would one day have to be caught like a rabid dog?

"Hank, what about Charlotte and the baby?" Little Luke was a year old now, but still Arlene thought of him as a baby.

"Violet won't hurt her sister or her nephew, and Lucas will be home from his ranch job up north. You don't have to worry about them."

"You don't know what Violet's like. She's so angry. She blames everyone for her unhappiness." She realized she was crying.

"If you're that worried, I'll have Lucas, Charlotte and Luke move in here with us. There's plenty of room."

Arlene felt sick. "You know why she escaped *now*, right before the wedding. She—"

"I won't let her stop the wedding."

She loved Hank more than life and knew how capable he was of taking care of her. But he didn't know

Violet and what *she* was capable of. Arlene did. "Maybe we should put off the wedding."

"No," Hank said. "If she isn't caught before the wedding, then I'll see that security is stepped up. I just want to make sure that you're safe until then. I'll be down to pick you up. Pack just what you need until the wedding. Has the storm hit there yet? It's snowing really hard up here. I think it's moving south in your direction, so bundle up."

"Hank—"

"Arlene, I'm not taking no for an answer. I'm on my way there now." He hung up.

Not that it would have made a difference to argue with him. She knew she couldn't talk him out of it, and maybe it would be best if she and Violet didn't cross paths right now. If Violet was upset about the wedding, there was no telling what she might do.

Arlene prayed that one day Violet could get well and live a normal life. But if she kept getting into trouble, she would never be released.

Going into the living room, Arlene walked over to the drapes and drew them back so she could look across the prairie as the sun crested the horizon—just as she had done for almost forty years.

AS DEDE DROVE THROUGH THE swirling snow, Lantry realized they were following the brunt of the storm south. The wind had kicked up, the temperature on the thermometer between the visors showing five below zero. He could no longer tell if it was snowing or if the snow in the air was being kicked up by the wind.

He hadn't seen a light for miles, and the secondary

road she'd taken was getting progressively worse. The pickup was bucking drifts. If it wasn't for catching sight of the top of an occasional fence post on each side of the barrow pit along the narrow, unpaved road, he would have doubted they were even still on a road.

"I'm curious," Dede said, breaking the silence. "What made you become a divorce lawyer?"

"Excuse me?"

"Don't you feel guilty taking advantage of two devastated people who are fighting for their lives?"

He growled under his breath, but settled back into the seat. "Don't you mean trying to kill each other over their *assets?* Not exactly their lives."

She shot him a scowl.

"Watch the road!" he said as the pickup hit a drift, snow cascading over the windshield.

"You've never been married, have you?" she said as visibility improved a little. "So you don't know what it's like to get divorced."

"Do we have to talk about this now? You really should be keeping your attention on the road." She had shifted into four-wheel low, the pickup slowly plowing its way through the snow. All he could figure was that she planned to cut across to Highway 191 once she was far enough south.

"Divorce is heartbreaking—even if you're the one who wants out of the marriage," she said as if he hadn't spoken. "When you get married, you have all these hopes and dreams—"

"Oh, please," Lantry snapped. "You married Frank because he was rich and powerful."

The moment the words were out, he regretted them—and not just because she touched the gun resting between her thighs. He had seen the wounded look on her face. He didn't want to be cruel, but he also couldn't take much more of this.

"I married Frank because I *loved* him," she said quietly.

"My mistake." He was glad when she put both hands back on the wheel.

"I guess I shouldn't be surprised you don't believe in love," Dede said, still sounding hurt.

Lantry warned himself to treat this woman with kid gloves. Who knew what she'd do next? And yet, she was so annoying. This whole situation was damned infuriating.

"It isn't love I don't believe in, it's marriage," he said into the hurt silence that had filled the pickup cab. "Any reasonable person who's seen the statistics would think twice before getting married, except that people in love always think they're going to be the ones who make it."

"But if you never gamble on love—"

"Marriage isn't a *gamble*. It's like playing Russian roulette with all but one of the chambers full of lead. Do you realize how many marriages end in divorce? Fifty percent of first marriages, sixty-seven percent of second marriages and seventy-four percent of third marriages."

"Have you always been this pessimistic?"

"Statistics don't lie," he said. "Most first marriages end after seven years. So do second marriages. Only thirty-three percent reach their twenty-fifth wedding anniversary. Half of all married people never reach their fifteenth anniversary. Only five percent make fifty years."

"I believed I was in that five percent."

"Even after what you'd been through?" He looked over at her as if she'd lost her mind, then remembered she had. "You thought Frank was the right person, which proves how blind love is. That's the reason why I am never getting married. My life is much safer without a spouse, and so are my assets."

She shot him a sympathetic look. "That's pitiful."

"I consider it intelligent."

"I still believe in marriage," she said stubbornly. "I've always loved those stories about married couples who die of old age within days of each other because the spouse can't stand to let the other one go without him or her."

He stared at her profile in the dash lights. "I'm astounded after your marriage to Frank that you can still wax romantic about marriage."

"When he put that gold band on my finger, I planned to wear it to my deathbed, the ring wearing thinner and thinner with the years." She shook her head. "I was wrong. But that doesn't mean that the institution of marriage is doomed."

He couldn't believe her, given what Frank had put her through. She actually had tears in her eyes.

"Come on, tell the truth. You pawned your engagement and wedding ring as quick as you could after the divorce without a second thought."

"I never even considered the monetary value."

"So where're the rings?" He saw her expression and burst out laughing. "You *did* pawn them."

"I had to use the rings to get out of the mental hospital in Texas. It was all I had to offer at the time."

She glanced over at him, then back at the road. "Why can't you believe that I loved Frank?"

That was the problem. He *did* believe it. What amazed him more than anything was that she *still* loved the man.

THROUGH THE FALLING AND BLOWING snow Violet could barely make out Old Town Whitehorse. The wind whipped the fallen snow into sculpted drifts, and the air outside the stolen SUV had an icy-cold weight to it that made it hard to breathe.

Violet cut the engine and stared down the hill at her mother's house. The day had turned bright with the earlier dawn and the falling snow.

"I don't understand what we're doing here," Roberta said. "Aren't the roads going to blow in? Maybe we should find some place to stay for a while."

"I'm going down to my house to get us some warmer clothes, food and money."

"What if your mother is home?" Roberta asked. "Maybe it's a trap."

That was the problem with hanging out with a schizophrenic.

Violet watched a large SUV pull into the drive. She picked up the binoculars she'd stolen along with clothing from one of the houses they'd visited earlier.

She watched a large man climb out and go into the house. A few minutes later, he came out with a suitcase, went back in and came out with a long garment bag and carefully put that into the backseat. Her mother's wedding gown?

A few moments later, her mother came out. She saw Arlene look around as if she knew Violet was close by. Maybe her mother knew her better than she'd thought.

Arlene seemed to hesitate as if she didn't want to leave. Finally, she got into the SUV and the two drove away. Violet had seen the man driving. The fiancé, no doubt. He looked…nice. Bigger and better looking than she'd expected.

Violet started to get out.

"You sure no one's home?" Roberta asked, looking down at the house through dim winter light. The temperature had dropped quickly inside the SUV while they'd been waiting.

Violet rolled her eyes. "Didn't you just see them drive off?"

"Still…"

"All the lights are off. They're gone, okay?" she snapped. She'd come to regret bringing Roberta along. "Stay here."

"What should I do if you don't come back?" Roberta asked.

"I *will* be back." Violet pulled the key from the ignition and climbed out. She was going home.

LANTRY WATCHED THE ROAD ahead—what little he could see of it—and listened to Dede talk about her marriage, trying to distract himself from thinking about what this woman might have planned for him.

"Frank changed," Dede was saying. "One day I just woke up, and I was lying next to a stranger."

"If I had a dollar for every time I've heard that," he said.

"I'm sure you got more than a dollar every time you heard it." The pickup broke through another large drift that had blown across the road. Fortunately, the roads out here were fairly straight since it was getting harder and harder to see where the roadbed lay between the fences.

"It made me wonder why Frank married me," she said.

That sexy body, Lantry thought but was smart enough not to say anything as she drove deeper into the storm and farther from civilization.

The snow was piling up. At least a foot had fallen and was still falling. The weather conditions were worsening to the point that he was becoming even more anxious. Where the hell was she taking him?

"You're going to love this," she said, "but I think Frank married me because I was so normal."

"Funny," he said. "You know you really don't seem like a woman who is running from killers."

"Because I made one little joke?"

"*Little* is right."

"Oh, I would have bet you had no sense of humor in your line of work."

"I'm a lawyer, not an undertaker."

"Right, you bury people alive."

"Could we discuss the reason you've kidnapped me instead of my chosen profession, please." He was having a hard time concentrating on the conversation. Snowflakes thick as cotton were blowing horizontally across the road, obliterating everything.

Dede had slowed the pickup to a crawl and now leaned over the steering wheel, straining to see.

"This is insane," he muttered under his breath. "You don't even know where you are."

He'd been watching the compass and temperature gauge in the pickup. The temperature outside had been steadily dropping as she drove south toward the Missouri Breaks—into no-man's-land—and the road was nearly drifted in.

If she planned to hook back up with Highway 191 south, she'd missed the turn.

"Dede—" He'd barely gotten the word out when a gust of wind hit the side of the pickup as the front of the truck broke through a large drift. The drift pulled the tires hard to the right.

Lantry felt the front tire sink into the soft snow at the edge of the road. Dede was fighting to keep the snow from pulling the pickup into the deeper snow of the barrow pit, but it was a losing battle.

Snow flew up over the hood and windshield as the truck plowed into the snow-filled ditch.

Lantry had seen it coming and braced himself. The pickup crashed through the deep snow, coming to an abrupt stop buried between the road and a line of fence posts and barbed wire.

He heard Dede smack her head on the side window since the pickup didn't have side air bags.

The only other sound was that of the gun clattering to the floorboard at his feet.

Chapter Three

Violet wasn't surprised to find the front door of the farm house unlocked. No one in these parts locked their doors—except when she was on the loose. Had her mother left the door open on purpose?

She gripped the knob as she pushed gently and the door swung in, the scents of her childhood rushing at her like ghosts from the darkness.

The brightness of the falling snow beyond the open curtains cast the interior of the house in an eerie pale light, making it seem even creepier, the memories all that more horrendous.

She stood for a moment, breathing hard in the dim light, then fumbled for the light switch. The overhead lamp came on, chasing away the shadows, forcing the ghosts to scurry back into their holes.

Violet moved quickly down the hall toward her old room and turned on the light. She hadn't expected her mother would keep her room exactly as it had been. She'd anticipated that Arlene might have boxed up her stuff and pushed it into a corner.

The room had been turned into a playroom for a child. Violet stared. She could tell that her mother had decorated the room. As she caught the scent of baby powder, she felt tears flood her eyes.

The realization hit her hard. Her mother had gotten rid of her—and her things. Arlene had never planned for her oldest daughter to come home again.

Violet swallowed the large lump in her throat only to have it lodge in her chest. There was nothing here for her.

"DEDE?"

She was slumped over, hands still gripping the wheel. "Dede?"

She lifted her head slowly, looking a little dazed as she shifted her gaze from the snow-packed windshield to him. "What happened?"

"We went in the ditch. Shut off the engine. The tailpipe's probably under the snow. The cab will be filling with carbon monoxide."

She took a hand off the wheel to rub her temple. It was red where she'd smacked it on the side window. Fumbling, she turned off the engine, pitching them into cold silence.

"Dede, you need to get these handcuffs off me."

She didn't move.

"We can't stay here. I saw a mailbox back up the road There must be a farmhouse nearby. If we stay here, we'll freeze to death. Do you understand what I'm saying?"

Her gaze went to her lap. He saw recognition cross her expression as she realized the gun was gone. She raised her eyes to him and saw that he'd managed to free the plastic cuffs from his belt, unsnap his seatbelt and retrieve the gun from where it had fallen on the floor-board. He'd stuck the gun in the waist band of his jeans.

"I wouldn't have shot you," she said quietly.

"I guess we're about to find out." He held out his cuffed wrists to her. "There's a hunting knife under the seat. I need you to cut these off. Unless you want to die right here in this barrow pit."

She met his gaze, held it for a moment, then reached under the seat, pulled the knife from its leather sheath and cut the plastic cuffs. Lantry rubbed his wrists, watching her as she put the knife back. She looked defeated, but he'd seen that look before and knew better than to believe it.

He tried his door. Just as he suspected, it wouldn't move. Snow was packed in around the truck. Dede's side, he saw, would be worse since snow was packed clear up past her window.

"We're going to have to climb out my side through the window. But first…" He turned to dig through the space behind the seats for what little spare clothing he carried. This was his first winter in Montana.

His stepmother, Kate, had lived here her first twenty-two years and knew about Montana winters. She'd told him numerous times to take extra clothing, water, a blanket and food each time he ventured off the ranch.

He wished now that he'd listened to her. All he had was a pair of snow pacs that he kept in the car in case he went off the road and a shovel in the bed of the truck in case he had to dig himself out.

There was no digging the pickup out of this ditch, especially in this blizzard. But at least his feet would be warmer in the pacs than in his cowboy boots.

He tugged off his boots and put on his pacs. All the time, he could feel Dede watching him, that desolate look in her eyes.

"You're going to turn me in," she finally said.

He looked up at her from tying the laces on the pacs. "We can figure things out once we get to the house back up the road."

He dug around behind the seat again and found an old hat with earflaps and a pair of worn work gloves. "Here, wear these. I'm afraid that's the best I can do." He glanced at her Santa suit. The feet on it were plush black fake fur with plastic soles.

"Give me your feet," he said. She eyed him with suspicion but did as she was told. Even with the thick fabric of the costume, he was able to slip his boots over it, making the cowboy boots fit well enough to get her to the house back up the road.

"Ready?" He pulled on his gloves, reached over and turned the key to put down his window. Snow cascaded in. He dug through the snow until he could see daylight and falling snow. "Come on."

"Is everything all right?" Roberta asked as Violet tossed an armload of clothing into the backseat, handed her a couple boxes of crackers and some salami and cheese, and slid behind the wheel.

"Perfect."

"Are those *your* clothes?"

"They're my mother's, if you must know. I had to

borrow a few of her things." Violet gave her a look, daring her to ask what had happened to her own clothes.

Roberta eyed her but was smart enough not to cross that line. "So what now?"

"We hang out until it's time to go to my mother's wedding shower, what else?" Violet snapped.

"Cool," Roberta said. "I love wedding showers."

Violet cut her eyes to her fellow escapee and questioned her own sanity for bringing Roberta along. True, Roberta had helped get the Santa costumes, since they weren't allowed real clothing on the criminally insane ward, and she had stood guard while Violet had stolen the SUV.

It had been Roberta's idea that they steal the Santa costumes for the upcoming Christmas show. "They will be warmer than our regulation hospital scrubs, and who is going to pull over three women dressed as Santas?" But Violet was beginning to think it was about time to ditch Roberta. All that kept her from it as she drove away from her former home was the fact that she might need Roberta in the near future.

"They say you're the company you keep," her dead grandmother said from the backseat with a chuckle. "In this case, two crazy peas in a pod."

"Shut up," Violet snapped.

Roberta looked over at her. "Your dead grandmother again?"

"That Roberta's a sharp one, all right," Grandma said. "Sharper than you, since going to your mother's shower is one of the dumbest things you've ever come up with. What's the point?"

Violet glared into the rearview mirror at her grandmother for a moment, then concentrated on the road. The snow was coming down so hard now that if she hadn't known the road, she would have ended up in the ditch.

She drove back to Whitehorse and turned onto the road to the Tin Cup. It surprised her how many cars were parked in the lot. She parked on the highway side on a small hill facing the large pond just off the road and cut the lights.

In the restaurant, she could see decorations hanging in front of the windows and people moving around behind the thin drapes.

"I thought we were going to a shower?" Roberta said.

Violet shot her a look. "We wait here for my mother."

"Then we follow her and run her off the road, drag her out of her car and beat her senseless," Roberta said with a smile. "How does that sound?"

Violet didn't answer as she helped herself to some of the neatly cut cheese and salami. It had been wrapped in the refrigerator, the boxes of crackers on the table with the note propped up against one of the boxes.

I'm sorry. The cheese and salami was all I had on hand.

Her mother had left her food, knowing she would come by the house. Knowing she would be hungry.

"Don't get all sentimental," her grandmother said from the backseat. "You should be in there at that party, eating that good food, not out here eating cheese and crackers."

The bite in her mouth turned to sawdust. Violet swallowed, hating that her grandmother was right. The unfairness of it all made her want to strike out at someone. That someone would have to be her mother.

DEDE DIDN'T TRUST LANTRY, BUT she didn't want to freeze to death in his pickup in a snowbank, either. She had little choice but to follow him. Lantry had the gun and, for the time being, she would have to go along with whatever he said.

She slithered out the window, crawling across the top of the wind-crusted drift to the edge of the road where Lantry lifted her up onto the more solid ground of the roadbed.

It was snowing harder than ever. The wind whipped the stinging icy flakes around her, freezing air biting at any bare flesh it could find.

"Cover your face and stay close," Lantry yelled over the wind as he motioned for her to follow him.

She squinted into the falling snow, then drew the costume up so only her eyes were uncovered. The cold and wind made her eyes tear. The boots on her feet made walking difficult.

Keeping to the tracks the pickup had made, she followed Lantry. But within a dozen yards, the wind had blown in the tracks and she found herself plowing through the drifts behind him, thankful for the moment that she wasn't alone out here in this storm.

Ducking her head against the bite of the snow and wind, she was at least glad for the thickness of the plush Santa suit and her hospital-issued cotton scrubs underneath. Following him, she put one foot in front of the other, trying not to think about the cold or her fear of what would happen once they reached the house he'd said would be back up the road.

Just as she'd done as a young girl, she counted her blessings to keep her mind off the cold and exhaustion that made each step a trial. At least she wasn't locked in a cage, and the men after her hadn't caught her. Yet.

That was as far as she could get on blessings. She was cold, tired, hungry, thirsty and scared. As badly as she couldn't wait to reach the house and get out of the bitter cold and snow, she dreaded getting anywhere that had a phone.

She didn't know how far they'd walked. She'd lost track of time, concentrating only on putting one foot in front of the other. The cold had numbed her senses, and she was beginning to believe Lantry had lied about seeing a mailbox, when he touched her arm, startling her since she hadn't realized he'd stopped.

He motioned for her to follow as he held two strands of barbed wire apart so she could climb through the fence. Then he broke a trail through the snow. Ahead, she caught a glimpse of a house through the driving snow and thought she might burst into tears with relief.

No lights glowed behind the windows of the two-story house. No Christmas decorations adorned the front yard or hung from the eaves. Was it possible the house was deserted? Just as she started to latch on to that hope, she heard a horse snort and saw three ghostlike shapes appear out of the storm next to a wooden corral fence.

The horses had a layer of snow on the quilted blankets covering their backs. As they trotted off, she saw that the road into the house was drifted in and didn't look as if it had been used for a while. Maybe the homeowners had only gone away for the holidays, leaving enough water and hay for the horses until they returned.

She slogged through the snow, the drifts to her thighs, the cold seeping into her bones. Just a little farther. She stumbled, her legs no longer willing to take another step.

As she felt herself start to sink down into the snow, her mind telling her she should sit down for a while and rest, Lantry picked her up and carried her the last two dozen yards to the porch. She leaned limply against him, her head on his shoulder, too exhausted to pick it up. She couldn't remember the last time she'd slept.

He set her down on the porch, but kept an arm around her. She hugged herself, shivering so hard that her teeth chattered. The sound of glass shattering made her jump. To her shock, Lantry had put his gloved fist through one of the small windows in the door and was now reaching in to unlock the door.

"You're breaking in?"

He shot her a look. "This from a woman who just pulled a gun on an officer of the law and left him locked in a jail cell?"

Had she not been so tired, she might have laughed at the incongruity of that. All thoughts evaporated as she felt a warm draft of air as Lantry opened the door and ushered her inside the wonderfully heated house.

She slumped down into a chair just inside as he closed the door behind them and tried the lights. "Good, we have electricity," he said as the reassuring glow of a lamp flashed on.

Her mind rallied long enough to form one clear thought: Did that mean they also had a phone? She still had his cell phone in the pocket of the costume. Had he forgotten about that?

She watched Lantry pick up a pillow from a nearby sofa and stuff it in the broken window before turning back to her.

She tried to still her trembling, but the effort was wasted. She could no longer feel her feet or fingers.

Without a word, he knelt down in front of her and pulled off the cowboy boots. Tossing them aside, he said, "Come on."

He pulled her to her feet and led her down the hall to a bathroom. She plopped down on the closed toilet seat as he turned on the shower. "It's not quite hot yet. I'm going to go find you something else to wear."

She nodded and didn't move.

He disappeared. She managed to get the cell phone out of her pocket and tried it. No signal. She'd barely gotten it back into the costume pocket before he returned with a stack of clothing.

"See if any of these fit you. Looks like the water's hot now. You can get in." As he started to leave the bathroom, he hesitated. She'd been trying to unzip the costume, only to find that her fingers no longer worked.

"Here, let me." He unzipped the Santa suit and helped her step out of it. Her feet were beet red, the same color as her hands. Under the suit she wore the blue scrubs required in her part of the mental hospital.

Lantry seemed to hesitate for a moment. "Can you manage the rest?"

She nodded and waited until he closed the door behind him. Steam rose from the shower, and she felt her brain starting to work again. She looked from the clothing he'd brought her to the bathroom window.

Even though her mind wasn't working to capacity, she knew that she couldn't make a run for it. Not in this storm. Not without proper warm clothing. Even if she knew the country well enough to find her way in the blizzard, she doubted she would survive.

But none of those reasons were why she couldn't make a run for her life. She had to convince Lantry. That's why she'd come here. Without his help…

She choked back a sob, feeling defeated and afraid as she slipped out of the scrubs. The heat from the shower had steamed up the bathroom, making it warm and close as she stepped in under the spray.

The water made her hands and feet ache, but she didn't care. Tears coursing down her cheeks, she turned her face up to the spray. The heat felt so good, she wished she could stay under the soothing water and never come out.

She knew she would have to tell Lantry the truth. She no longer had any other option. And what if she couldn't convince him?

She stood under the water a little longer, then shut it off and reached for a towel. By now Lantry would have called his brother. Time was running out—and not just for her.

LANTRY WAITED UNTIL HE HEARD the shower running before he checked the cell phone he'd taken from the Santa costume. Just as he'd feared. No service this far south of Whitehorse. This whole part of Montana had only pockets of cell-phone service around the towns.

He found a landline in the kitchen, but the moment

he picked it up and heard the buzzing, he knew the storm had taken out the line. Happened all the time out here. He was surprised the electricity was still on.

No way to call for help. Not that help could probably get to them until the plows ran. He checked the time, shocked at how many hours had gone by. It was afternoon already, the light beginning to fade.

When he turned on the radio, all he could get was the static-filled local station. A Christmas carol ended, and the announcer broke in to say that all roads out of Whitehorse were closed due to the storm. Everyone was advised to stay inside. Only emergency travel was advised in Whitehorse because of poor visibility and dangerous road conditions.

"In other news, residents are to be on the lookout for three state mental-hospital inmates who have escaped and are believed to be in the area. At least one of the inmates, Violet Evans, is considered dangerous. Anyone who should see the escapees is advised to call the sheriff's department at once. Do not try to apprehend any of three."

Another Christmas carol came on. The announcer apparently didn't have the updated news about Dede and the hostage situation.

The wind howled at the windows, sending a shower of snow off the eaves, reminding him how far they were from Whitehorse. This country was so isolated, its own form of wilderness. They'd been lucky that a ranch house had been only a couple of miles back up the road. If they'd gone off a little farther to the south…

He shoved that thought away and stepped to the fireplace to build a fire from the stack of wood piled next to it. The house had felt warm at first, but now there was a chill in the room. He wondered if it was from the temperature dropping further—or from his own chilling thoughts.

Had either phone been working, he would have turned Dede in. He told himself it wasn't a question of whether he believed her or not. He was an officer of the court. She was wanted by the authorities. Of course, he would turn her over to them.

So why was he wasting time even thinking about it?

On the radio, there was another bulletin about the roads and the escapees. "The police believe they will try to seek shelter. Residents are advised to keep their houses and cars locked and stay inside."

The dry wood in the stone fireplace began to crackle, flames leaping warmly. He started at a sound and turned to find Dede standing behind him.

She looked so small, so vulnerable, so scared. But amazingly, she also looked softer, sweeter, if that were possible, her cheeks glowing from the hot shower.

From the look on her face, she'd heard the announcement.

"The phone's out, there's no cell coverage out this way and all the roads out of Whitehorse are closed," he said, wondering why he was so quick to reassure her of her safety—at least for the moment.

Her relief was palpable.

"The clothes fit all right?"

She nodded, and he tried not to notice the way the jeans hugged her bottom or the rust-colored sweater accentuated her curves as she stepped to the fire.

"The people who live here must have gone away for

the holidays," Lantry said to her back. "I noticed when we came in that they left hay and plenty of water for the horses."

Her stomach growled loudly.

He couldn't help but grin. "Hungry?"

Her stomach growled again in answer. "Is there food?"

"This is rural Montana. There is always food. Why don't you check the kitchen while I see about bringing in more wood."

She nodded with a self-conscious smile. "I *am* a little hungry."

He watched her head for the kitchen, shuffling in the too-large slippers he'd found for her.

He listened to her opening and closing cabinets as he pulled on his coat. As he slogged out to the woodpile through the drifts, the wind whipped snow around him. He bent his head to it, grabbed up an armload of wood and headed back toward the house.

As he caught a glimpse of Dede through the kitchen window, it hit him. They were stranded—at least until a snowplow could get down this road. Primary roads would get plowed first, and with all the roads out of Whitehorse closed, it could be days before this road was open.

He was trapped here with a woman who both scared and fascinated him. A woman he couldn't trust—and yet wanted to. He was in dangerous territory, he thought, glancing again toward the kitchen window and Dede.

Chapter Four

Dede heard the front door bang open, felt the cold draft of air rush in as Lantry stomped his snow boots, slammed the door and dropped the armload of wood next to the fire.

She glanced toward the living room and saw him warming his hands in front of the fireplace. He looked so pensive. So deep in thought. She didn't kid herself that had the phones been working, he would have sold her down the river in a heartbeat.

She couldn't trust this man. No matter how considerate he'd been to her.

"Did you find something for us to eat?" Lantry called without looking in her direction.

The cupboards were filled with canned goods, and the freezer was full of beef. "Yes," she called back. She had taken two T-bone steaks from the freezer and put them in the microwave to defrost and was now considering which of many home-canned vegetables to prepare with the steaks when she heard him come into the kitchen.

She could feel him studying her as she heard him pull out a chair and sit down at the big oak table.

"I thought we'd have steak and baked potatoes. I found some butter and sour cream in the fridge. But I can't decide between canned green beans and canned corn," she said, turning to look at him.

His smile softened the hard lines of his face. He really was an amazingly attractive man. "How about both? I'm starved." He stretched out his long legs.

"Me, too," she said as her stomach growled again. She glanced at the clock, and realized why she was so hungry. She hadn't had anything to eat since supper the day before at the hospital—almost twenty-four hours ago.

She took the steaks from the microwave and popped in two large potatoes to cook. The cast-iron skillet she'd put on the stove with butter melting in it was hot enough that she dropped in the steaks.

"I wouldn't have taken you for a woman who cooked," Lantry said behind her.

She bristled at the remark. "That's because you don't know anything about me," she said without turning around. "You made a lot of erroneous assumptions about me based on what your client told you, and since you weren't interested in the truth—"

His laugh made her break off in midsentence.

She turned to find him grinning at her.

"You're right," he said and held up his hands in surrender.

"What does that mean?" she asked suspiciously as the steaks sizzled in the skillet.

"You're right, and since we have nothing but time,

after dinner I want you to tell me everything about you and what's really going on."

She narrowed her gaze at him, studying him. "And you'll listen with an open mind?"

He pushed himself to his feet. "You have my word," he said as he moved to the cupboards. He opened one, then another, before he found the dishes. He began to set the table. In the other room, the radio played "Deck the Halls."

They ate at the table to the glow of the fire in the next room. Music played softly on the radio. The house felt warmer. Or maybe it was just sitting across from this man, Dede thought as she devoured the food.

"I can't remember anything tasting this good," she said as she finished.

"I know what you mean. I didn't realize how hungry I was. Good job on the steaks."

"You make me nervous when you're nice to me," she said, studying him. She'd expected him to laugh. Or at least grin. But he did neither.

He looked at her with compassion. "I'm sorry you feel that way. I never wanted to be unkind to you."

The food had helped fight off some of her exhaustion, but she knew it wouldn't last. She had to convince him to help her before the snowplows opened the road.

AFTER THEY'D CLEANED UP THE kitchen, Lantry threw more logs on the fire and they sat down at separate ends of the couch in front of the blaze. He felt full and strangely content—all things considered. Dede seemed lost in her own thoughts.

He wanted to give her the benefit of the doubt. Now more than ever, he felt he owed her that. He'd helped Frank push her to this breaking point. And while all of that was true, he knew the main reason he wanted to hear her out was because he was beginning to like her.

The woman had a strength that amazed him. She'd been through so much, and yet there was still a whole lot of fight in her. He thought about her trudging through the snowdrifts in that damned Santa suit and smiled to himself. He'd seen the exhaustion on her face. The cold had weakened even him.

She'd been facing ultimate defeat, but she'd kept going, knowing that if the phone had worked once they reached the ranch house, he'd have turned her in.

He felt guilty about that now. He'd been ready to throw her to the wolves without even hearing her out. Of course, she had taken him from the jail at gunpoint, he reminded himself as the fire crackled softly.

Dede sat for a moment, staring into the fire, before she said, "I haven't been completely honest with you."

Lantry looked over, saw Dede's face and felt sick. Hadn't he had a feeling that Dede wasn't telling him everything?

"I told you that Frank called me at the hospital in Texas. He told me things had gotten out of his control and that my life was in danger. He told me to do whatever I had to, but to get out of there and run."

"Why didn't you take his advice?"

"Because I knew my husband." She looked at him with those big blue innocent eyes, and he felt the pull of this woman, stronger than the fiercest tides. "I knew his secret. I overhead him on the phone one night before the divorce. I hadn't meant to be eavesdropping." She hesitated. "I feel disloyal telling this even now."

Dede took a breath and let it out slowly. "I heard Frank say he wanted out. Whoever was on the other end of the line was arguing with him. Frank said, 'There has to be a price for my freedom, dammit.' Then he fell silent. I could see his shadow on the wall. He had his head in his hand. After he hung up, I heard him crying." Her voice broke, and she got up to stand with her back to him in front of the fire.

"After that, Frank was a different man—cold, hateful. I tried to talk to him…" Her voice trailed off, and for a while, there was only the crackle of the fire and her fragile dark silhouette against the flames.

"You said you knew Frank's secret. Is that why these men are after you?" Lantry asked, rising to put more wood on the fire.

"Frank had something they wanted." She raised her gaze to his, the two of them standing inches apart as the fire roared softly in the chilly room.

"What would make you think that?" he asked, feeling a little lightheaded. It was hard not to be completely entranced by that angelic face and those eyes of hers. This close, he could smell the fresh scent of the soap on her skin, in her hair.

"Look what they did to the house. You didn't really think I would destroy a seven-thousand-dollar couch like that, did you?"

He recalled the photographs Frank had shown him. Photographs of the house torn apart as if by a madman. Or a furious, crazed wife. He'd been shocked by the destruction. So had the doctor who'd signed Dede's commitment papers at Frank's urging.

"Insane or simply angry, who has the energy to ransack every room of a twelve-thousand-square-foot house?" she asked.

"Frank must have known who destroyed your house," Lantry said. "Why would he lie and say you did?"

"I told you. Frank *loved* me. He thought I would be safe locked up where no one would believe anything I said. He was trying to protect me."

Lantry would have argued that, but one look in the depths of those blue eyes of hers and he couldn't bring himself to raise a word of protest. "You don't have to pretend with me."

"Pretend what?"

"That he didn't break your heart."

DEDE WAITED FOR THAT AWFUL ache to form in her chest. To her surprise, she felt only a slight flutter, nothing more. She should have been relieved that it didn't hurt as much as it had, but instead she was filled with an odd sense of regret.

Frank was gone. Not just from her life, but from her heart. That made her sad. She'd planned to spend the rest of her life with him. Maybe Lantry was right about love and marriage. Maybe nothing lasted, not love, not even the pain of a broken heart.

"Dede, I can see how hard even talking about this is for you," Lantry said quietly. "I'm sorry. I hate the part I played in what's happened to you."

She stared at Lantry, unable to hide her surprise. He continued to keep her off balance.

She'd despised Lantry Corbett from the moment Frank had hired him and she'd heard how ruthless he was.

She'd heard he was an amazing lawyer but a man without a conscience, a poor excuse for a human being. She'd told herself there had to be more to Lantry Corbett than what she'd heard about him.

But on meeting him, she'd been devastated to discover that apparently what she'd heard about him was true. He seemed cold, calculating and with no regard for truth or justice.

So how did she explain what appeared to be this change in him? Or had there been this man inside the divorce lawyer all along? More to the point, could she trust him?

"I suspect you like letting people believe you're a heartless bastard," she said, not unkindly.

He smiled at that. "I suppose I do. But I don't like myself as I see me reflected in your eyes."

She wished he wasn't so devastatingly handsome, especially on those rare occasions when his smile reached his eyes.

"It *is* hard for me to talk about this, but you have to know everything," she said. "I'm ashamed to say that I didn't just eavesdrop on Frank. After the change in him, I listened in on his phone calls, I checked his pockets, went through his wallet, hired a private detective. That's when I found out his secret."

VIOLET FELT SOMETIMES AS IF her skin were too tight. As if her own body had turned against her like everyone else had. As if she were killing herself slowly.

"Crazy thought," she warned herself silently.

"Not so crazy," her dead grandmother said from the backseat as they waited for the wedding shower to let out. "I told your mother again and again that there was something wrong with you. Did she listen? Of course not. No one ever listens to me. Just like you. You don't listen to me, do you, Violet? If you'd have listened to me, all this would be over. But no, you just had to do things your way."

Violet covered her ears, but she could still hear her grandmother's voice. "Shut up! SHUT UP!"

Roberta's curly head popped up from the passenger seat, where she'd been sleeping as the blizzard raged around the stolen SUV. She blinked, looking around in confusion. "What's going on?" she demanded hoarsely.

Violet took her hands from her ears and glanced in the rearview mirror to where her grandmother had been sitting only moments before. "Nothing."

"Then who the hell were you yelling at?" Roberta wanted to know.

"No one. It was just—"

"Not your grandmother again," Roberta said, glancing around the interior of the stolen SUV. "You should have driven a stake through her heart when she died. Otherwise they come back, you know."

Violet knew only too well. Her grandmother had been coming back for some time now. In fact, it was her grandmother who'd kept Violet from getting out of the mental hospital. She'd been so close to being released.

She'd convinced the doctor that she was well, that she could make it on the outside—until her grandmother started nagging at her, just as she had in life.

"Go back to sleep," she told Roberta. Not that it was necessary. The woman had already curled up and was snoring softly.

Violet wished she could sleep like that. The SUV rocked in the wind, and snow swirled around it. Violet had started the engine and turned the heater on high as she waited for her mother's wedding shower to end. It should be soon, given the storm.

She'd always hated winter and used to dream of moving to somewhere warm. Maybe that's what she'd do once she was free of the past. Before she went, she should go up to the cemetery in Old Town Whitehorse where her grandmother was buried and dig up the old biddy and put a stake through her heart.

As if listening in on her thoughts, her grandmother leaned forward and began to whisper horrible things in her ear.

Violet tried desperately not to listen. But in the end, she couldn't keep the words from gnawing their way in.

Stop being that poor old-maid daughter of Arlene Evans and show them what you can do. Make it so no one in the county ever forgets the name Violet Evans.

LANTRY LIFTED AN EYEBROW AS IF he realized what it had taken Dede to hire a private investigator to spy on her husband.

"There was another woman," Lantry guessed.

Dede nodded. "Frank had been meeting with a

woman named Tamara Fallon. They were clearly close, probably having an affair, although the only photographs the private investigator was able to get was of them arguing and later hugging outside a restaurant.

"I know that doesn't prove anything," she said, hurrying on before Lantry could point out the obvious. "Clearly the two were involved in some way, and that was enough for me."

"Don't tell me you didn't try to fight for your marriage and your husband."

"You think you know me." She smiled ruefully and shook her head. "No sexy nightgown or romantic dinner was going to get my husband back. I needed information. The name Fallon had sounded familiar. I realized I'd seen it somewhere recently—but not in any of Frank's e-mails or correspondence. I found the name in the newspaper. Tamara Fallon and her husband, Dr. Eric Fallon, had recently been burglarized."

Lantry let out a low curse. She had his attention now. "Some very expensive jewelry had been taken. I remember the story in the newspaper, now that you mention it. A diamond necklace was taken that was said to be worth over a million dollars."

"What wasn't in the newspapers was that the Fallons were in the process of having a new security system installed. The P.I. had discovered that Frank had been in the security-system business before he met me. A woman named Tammy Lundgren had been his bookkeeper."

"Tamara Fallon is Tammy Lundgren."

She nodded. "Even more interesting, the reason

Frank's business had folded was that he was being investigated because of a string of burglaries in houses where they'd either put in the security systems or had bid on the projects."

"Let me guess. You confronted Frank with what you'd learned."

"He denied everything." The memory still hurt her. "He told me I was crazy for even suspecting he might be involved with another woman—or in anything illegal."

"And, of course, you told him about the private investigator and showed him the photos of him and Tammy."

It annoyed her that she'd obviously done what other women faced with divorce had done.

"I wanted to help him, and as long as he kept denying there wasn't a problem…" She shrugged. "A mistake in retrospect."

"He had to have tried to explain the incriminating snapshots of him and Tammy Fallon."

"Frank said Tammy had called him out of the blue. She was having marital problems and needed a shoulder to cry on. Frank swore he told her he couldn't help her. Which could explain why they appeared to be arguing in the photos. He was furious that I'd spied on him and, worse, thought he was having an affair. He said he hadn't heard from her since."

"Did you believe him?"

Dede shrugged. "Things only got worse between us after that. Frank would get calls from either Ed or Claude. I would hear him arguing with them. And sometimes I would answer the phone and the party on the other end would hang up."

"You think Frank had something to do with the Fallon burglary?"

"Why would he risk everything? He was successful. He had a reputation to uphold in Houston. He didn't need the money."

"Unless these people from his past had some kind of leverage over him."

She nodded slowly. "But if that was the case, then I fear Frank double-crossed them."

A loud noise outside the ranch house made them both start.

Chapter Five

Violet turned on the wipers and leaned forward in the driver's seat, her dead grandmother forgotten as she watched people come out of the Tin Cup.

The snow wasn't as deep, the storm as strong, here in the Milk River Valley as it had been farther to the south nearer the Little Rockies. But of the several dozen vehicles parked around the restaurant on the hill, all covered with snow and virtually indistinguishable, which one was her mother's? Maybe the rich fiancé had lent Arlene that big SUV he'd picked her up in earlier.

She gripped the wheel as she saw the figure of her mother, arms full of presents and flanked by other women carrying even more gifts, hurrying out. Arlene Evans hadn't gone far when one of the SUVs parked on the edge of the road started up and drove toward her.

"The fiancé?" Violet barely got the words out of her mouth when the driver flashed his headlights and Arlene was caught in the glare. A thought struck Violet like a punch: her mother looked happy. She couldn't ever remember her mother being happy.

Violet swore as she watched the man get out and help Arlene load all her presents into the car. Seeing how happy her mother was, seeing this man come to rescue his woman, all of it filled Violet with conflicting emotions that roiled inside her.

"Something wrong?" Roberta asked, blinking as she sat up and looked down at all the lights from the vehicles leaving the party.

"I should have known he'd pick her up," Violet said as she shifted into gear but didn't turn on the head-lights. "This is even better than I planned. We'll take out both of them."

Roberta shrugged her disinterest. "I thought we were going to chase her down and pull her out of her car and—"

"You might want to buckle up," Violet interrupted as she slammed her foot down on the gas. She had posi-tioned the stolen SUV in just the right spot. Ahead she had a clear view of the road out to the highway.

"This is another one of your bad ideas," Grandma said from the backseat. "Pure self-indulgence, and what is it going to accomplish, huh?"

"Satisfaction, you old hag," Violet snapped and hit the gas, anticipating the moment her mother saw her behind the wheel—the moment of impact.

AT THE SOUND OUTSIDE, LANTRY moved to the front window to part the curtains and look out. A large plastic garbage container cartwheeled through the snow to disappear over a rise.

Just for a moment, all Dede's gloom and doom about their lives being in danger had seemed real. Too real.

Lantry realized he was tired and irritable from lack of sleep, worn thin from the cold and this situation.

"While all this is fascinating, Dede," he said as he turned from the window, his heart still jumping a little, "it doesn't explain why anyone would want either of us dead."

"I told you Frank called me at the mental hospital in Texas. What I didn't tell you was that Frank told me he was in serious trouble. He'd left a package with someone he had to get back. If he didn't, they were going to kill him. If Frank had something to leave for safekeeping, he would have left it with someone he trusted."

Lantry realized where she was going with this. "If you're thinking he left this package with me—"

"Frank trusted you. You'd done well for him. He had to have given it to you. I'm not the only one who believes that. What other reason could there be for these men to want you dead?"

Lantry shook his head, remembering the last time he'd seen Frank Chamberlain. Frank had kept looking at his watch, complaining about the air-conditioning being too low and mopping his brow. He'd been nervous as hell and had made a point of sitting facing the door.

He'd thought Frank was worried Dede would show up and make a scene or, worse, shoot him.

Maybe that's all it had been.

Or maybe Dede was right. Frank had been between a

rock and a hard place because of Tammy Fallon—and because his wife had found out about his past. A man with secrets, some of which were coming to light. Did that explain why he'd had Dede put in a mental institution?

"If Frank had left some package with someone, why didn't he just go get it himself?"

She shook her head. "I've tried reaching him, but there hasn't been any answer, and his voice mail is full."

Lantry didn't like the sound of this and could tell that Dede was worried about her ex. Had Frank tried to call him? When Lantry had taken his leave of absence from the business, he'd had his secretary, Shirley, shield him from all the day-to-day business.

Shirley was a bulldog when it came to protecting him from stressed-out, erratic clients, since almost all divorce clients were on the emotional edge.

"I'm sorry, but Frank didn't give me anything." That in itself was a little odd now that Lantry thought about it.

His clients often gave him "thank-you" gifts. Usually a bottle of rare Scotch or bourbon or a box of expensive chocolates. Frank Chamberlain hadn't even thanked him.

"Frank wouldn't have just *given* it to you. He would have hid it in a gift or—"

"He didn't give me *anything*," Lantry said, seeing that she had pinned all her hopes on this.

Dede looked crestfallen and uncertain. "I was so sure…"

Lantry couldn't say what made him do it—even later when he had too much time to think about it. She'd just looked so crushed he hadn't been able to help himself. He had smelled the scent of the soap, her hair still damp, the cap of curls framing that angelic face and those big blue eyes filled with pleading…. He'd weakened.

He hooked a hand around her slim neck and pulled her to him. Her blue eyes widened in surprise. His gaze went to her mouth, the full lips trembling slightly as he dropped his mouth to hers.

The kiss was gentle and soft, tender, the taste of her as sweet as he'd imagined it would be.

THE VEHICLE CAME OUT OF THE storm running full bore, no headlights, no chance to avoid it.

Arlene saw the cloud of snow an instant before the SUV came flying out at her. She screamed. Hank sped up. The vehicle missed Arlene's door and instead glanced off the back rear panel of Hank's bigger SUV, the impact jolting Arlene into silence.

The force of the crash spun them around and into the deep snow at the edge of the frozen pond. The big SUV came to a rest at an odd angle.

"Hank?" Arlene cried as she looked over at her fiancé. He unsnapped his seat belt and reached under the seat, coming out with a pistol as the vehicle that had hit them sped off down the road to the highway.

"Hank! No!" she cried, grabbing his arm as he started to open his door and get out.

He met her gaze, held it for a moment, then put the gun back under the seat and slid over to take her in his arms.

"Are you all right?" he whispered against her hair.

"I'm fine." She shuddered. Her world felt as if it had fallen away, leaving her teetering with no solid ground.

"It was Violet." Her eldest daughter. The daughter that had resembled her. The daughter she'd failed.

She began to cry. Hank unsnapped her seat belt and took her in his arms, the only place she'd ever felt safe.

"It's going to be all right," Hank whispered. "I promise you. It's going to be all right."

But Arlene knew better.

"I should have taken more precautions," Hank was saying.

"We have to postpone the wedding."

"No. No one is going to keep me from marrying you. You have my word on that. Violet isn't going to spoil this for us."

Arlene felt the lights of the other vehicles coming from the party wash over them.

"Do you believe me?" Hank asked.

"You don't know Violet. She won't stop until—"

He looked into her eyes, forcing her to meet the intensity of his gaze. "You and I are getting married Saturday."

She stared into his handsome face and felt his strength in the arms around her. She nodded as she heard car doors slam and people calling to them. Everyone would know soon enough that Violet was on the loose again. God help them all.

LANTRY SEEMED TO COME TO HIS SENSES almost at once.

"We should get some sleep," he said to Dede as he drew back from the kiss, his thumb skimming over her porcelain cheek.

She nodded slowly but said nothing. Her tongue

touched her upper lip. She couldn't believe he'd just kissed her.

Dede shivered, hugging herself, chilled by the surge of emotions coursing through her.

She'd *wanted* him to kiss her. Wanted him to take her in his arms and hold her. She silently cursed herself. She'd been ready to fall into Lantry Corbett's arms.

That just proved how desperate she felt. How afraid. Lantry Corbett was still the divorce lawyer who everyone said would eat his own young.

It was just hard to remember that since it had been a good-looking, lanky cowboy who'd just kissed her. And worse, she'd always had a weakness for cowboys.

And when Lantry was kind and compassionate toward her, she had let down all her defenses. Worse, she'd welcomed the comfort of his kiss, his arms around her.

He tossed more wood on the fire and straightened, looking uneasy. "We're both exhausted and not thinking straight."

She nodded, but she knew it was over. Even if the phone lines stayed down for another day or so, the plows would come through in the morning and see Lantry's pickup in the ditch. It was just a matter of time before she was behind bars—or, worse, on her way back to the mental hospital, where Claude would be waiting for her.

She'd been so sure Frank had given whatever it was he'd been hiding to Lantry. The worst part was that Ed and Claude also believed Lantry had it. Just as they believed she knew something and had become a threat they weren't willing to live with.

As she looked at Lantry, she realized that she'd failed not only Frank, but now this cowboy.

LANTRY FELT A CHILL AT THE defeated look on Dede's face. "We'll figure something out in the morning."

A rueful smile curled her lips as her gaze met his.

"I'm not going to turn you in."

She shook her head. "I heard the weather report on the radio."

He had wondered if she'd heard it earlier. Apparently she had.

"In the morning, the blizzard will have stopped. A plow will come down that road and see your pickup. I'm sure your brother already has everyone in the county looking for you—just like you said." She sighed. "We both know I'll be on my way back to the mental hospital before the sun sets."

She started to turn away, but he touched her arm to turn her back to him.

He tried to find some words of comfort for her, but was at a loss. All of this had him feeling confused and unsure. He could see how much she was counting on him having whatever package Frank might have left behind. Her worry for Frank still amazed him.

"We'll figure something out in the morning," he repeated and saw disappointment well in her eyes before she turned away again.

She was right about all of it. He was counting on them being found in the morning. At first he'd told himself that all of this was merely the fictional fabric of Dede Chamberlain's demented mind.

He no longer believed that. Dede needed help all right, but not the kind she would get at the mental hospital. He would do everything in his power to get her out of there. Once he'd told Shane everything Dede had told him about Frank and the Fallon burglary...

It wouldn't be easy without some kind of proof, though, and unfortunately Lantry knew only too well how slowly the legal system's wheels turned. If he believed Dede, that her life was in danger—maybe especially in the mental hospital—then how could he let her be taken back there?

He should never have kissed her. He questioned his judgment. Had he bought in to all of this because of that face of hers? Those eyes? The way she looked at him with all that hope?

Frank hadn't given him anything for safekeeping. Dede was mistaken. How much more was she mistaken about?

He heard her moving around upstairs in the bedroom he'd told her she could use. He heard the creak of the bedsprings, then silence. She wasn't crazy enough to try to make a run for it in this weather, was she?

But maybe freezing to death in the storm was the least of Dede Chamberlain's worries.

If she wasn't delusional, if someone really was trying to kill her, then sending her back to the mental hospital was a death sentence.

So how could he send her back there? And if she was right, then he'd better start worrying about his own hide, he thought with a curse as he remembered what his friend had told him about the steering mechanism on the Lamborghini.

Frowning, he moved to the window and pulled back the curtains to stare out at the storm.

You were his lawyer. You got him everything he wanted in the divorce. He trusted you.

Dede had asked him if Frank had given him something. He realized it had been a lie when he'd said no.

Frank *had* given him something. A wake-up call. Now, after all these years of living up to his reputation as a cold-blooded, merciless lawyer, it had come back to haunt him.

Snow blew past the window horizontally to pile in drifts along the road. An even bigger storm raged inside him.

Dede was right. A snowplow would be coming through sometime tomorrow. The driver would see the pickup in the ditch. It would be just a matter of time before the sheriff's department would be notified and he and Dede would be found.

Even with a lot of legal maneuvering, he wouldn't be able to keep Dede from being sent back to the mental hospital—at least temporarily. A mental evaluation would be required to decide if she should be charged with the incident at the jail.

He shook his head as he dropped the curtain and went back to the fire to curl up on the couch. As exhausted as he was, he knew he wouldn't be getting any sleep, not with his thoughts as wild as the weather raging outside the farmhouse.

What the hell was he going to do come morning?

DEPUTY SHERIFF SHANE CORBETT found everyone in the family waiting for him the next morning at the main house on Trails West Ranch. Everyone except his brother Lantry.

"Any word?" his father asked the moment he walked in.

Shane shook his head. "I came as soon as the road opened. All I know is what I told you on the phone earlier. Lantry was last seen with the wife of one of his clients from Texas."

"We heard on the radio that she is one of the three women who escaped from the state mental hospital— the criminally insane ward," his father's wife, Kate, said.

Shane cursed the media and its need to know and report everything. "She was only being held in that ward because she'd escaped from a mental hospital in Texas. She apparently had a breakdown during her divorce from one of Lantry's clients."

"If Lantry was her husband's lawyer…" Kate's voice broke.

"We have no reason to believe she will harm him," Shane said, wishing that were true.

Juanita pressed a mug of hot coffee into his hands. He took it, smiling his thanks at the family cook. He cradled the mug in his two large hands, trying to soak up the warmth—and hide how worried he was about his brother.

"I can't stay. We have all our deputies out looking for the escapees and Lantry," he said. "They couldn't have gotten far, not in that blizzard last night. More than likely they holed up somewhere to wait out the storm and will pay hell getting out with the roads blown in the way they are. We'll find them."

"Wouldn't Lantry have called if he'd got in out of the storm?" Russell asked. He was the oldest of the Corbett brothers and known as the most levelheaded.

"The phone lines were down for most of the county," Shane said. He didn't say that Dede Chamberlain was armed and might not have let Lantry make a call. If he was still alive.

He shook off that thought and took a sip of the hot coffee, burning his tongue.

"Lantry can take care of himself," the youngest of the brothers said. Jud, like his twin, Dalton, had been quiet since Shane's arrival. He'd seen the worry in all of his brothers' faces. The details of Lantry's abduction from the jail hadn't been released, but Shane had learned that nothing stayed a secret long in this small town.

"Jud's right. Lantry can take care of himself," Shane agreed. While no one had mentioned it, Shane suspected they all knew that Dede had taken the new deputy's weapon and abducted Lantry at gunpoint last night. That suspicion was verified a moment later.

"The man's a *divorce* lawyer. I'm sure this isn't the first time someone's held a gun on him," Jud joked, clearly trying to lighten the mood in the room. "He can certainly handle a woman."

"I should get going," Shane said and drank a little more of the coffee.

As he started to leave, the lights of the Christmas tree caught his eye. It was a huge ponderosa pine. The entire family had taken the hay wagon into the Breaks to cut it down, then come back to the ranch to decorate it.

Shane thought of the laughter and that safe feeling

he'd felt being a part of this family. Especially with his fiancée, Maddie, at his side.

They'd been through so much this year. Three weddings, some close calls, the revelation of a long-held secret.

This Christmas was to be a celebration as well as a time to give thanks for all their blessings and being together.

But now Lantry was somewhere with a mentally deranged woman with a gun and a grudge. He feared for Lantry's life and the devastation of his family if something tragic should happen to his brother.

His father walked him to the door. Grayson looked older and grayer, worry etched in his face. "Be careful, son. I heard this morning about that one escapee running her mother and her mother's fiancé off the road last night."

"Violet Evans," Shane said like a curse. Violet had gotten away, but fortunately neither Arlene Evans or Hank Monroe had been hurt. Now, though, everyone knew Violet was in town—and dangerous.

"It sounds like you've got too many nuts out there just looking for trouble," Grayson said.

Shane smiled at his father's concern. "I'll watch out for them, don't worry." He put a hand on his father's still-broad shoulder. "I'll call as soon as I find Lantry."

LANTRY DOZED OFF JUST BEFORE dawn and woke with a start. For a moment he didn't know where he was. He listened, the quiet so intense it was oppressive. Sitting up, he looked toward the window. Through a crack in the curtains, he could see that the storm had stopped. Snow was piled high against the window.

It came back in a rush. His gaze shot to the spot on the couch where the gun had been next to him.

Gone.

Lantry shot to his feet and rushed up the stairs, afraid he knew what had awakened him. At the second-floor landing, he slowed, trying to still his racing fear as well.

She wouldn't take off on her own.

She wasn't that stupid. Or that crazy.

Also, she'd begged for his help.

If she was telling the truth, she'd stick around and see if he could save her.

Even as he thought it, he knew. Once it got light and the storm ended, she had known what was going to happen. He'd told her he wouldn't turn her in, but she'd known that wouldn't matter. Once his pickup was spotted, it was only a matter of time before they'd be found and her butt was in the back of a van headed for the mental-hospital lockdown and…

He'd reached the closed door to her room and stopped. Even as he grabbed the knob, cautiously turned it and pushed open the door, he knew she was gone before he saw the empty bed.

Still he called "Dede?" as he stepped in. The bathroom door was open. No Dede.

Swearing, he turned and raced back down the stairs, thinking she might be in the kitchen. Yeah, right— armed and cooking breakfast for him.

The kitchen was empty. No big surprise. Dede Chamberlain was long gone.

Chapter Six

Lantry hurried to the front door and looked out, figuring she would head for the road but wouldn't be able to get far.

There would be tracks in the fresh snow. She would be easy to follow, and he had no doubt he could catch up to her.

He was sure he had only dozed off for a short while early this morning before the storm had stopped. Dede wouldn't have left until the storm was over, because she wasn't a fool. In fact, she seemed a hell of a lot smarter than him right now.

He opened the front door and looked out, surprised to see there were no tracks in the perfect, marblelike sculpted snow. The morning light glistened off the wind-crusted surface. Dede hadn't gone out this way.

At the back door, he found her footprints and followed them. They led right to the barn. Beyond it, he saw the horses and remembered Dede's reaction last night at dinner when he'd asked "Do you ride?" after seeing her watching the horses through the window.

"No." She'd shuddered. "I don't ride." He'd glimpsed what he'd thought was her fear of horses.

She'd lied.

He thought about catching one of the horses and going after her, but he knew she would have too much of a lead on him on horseback. As he listened, he could hear the sound of a snowplow in the distance.

As he trudged back through the snow, he couldn't help but wonder how much more of Dede's story had been a lie. He was furious with her. But mostly with himself.

After all these years of being a lawyer, a divorce lawyer who knew from the jump that there was always another side to any story in a marriage, he'd bought into her sad tale.

He cursed himself as he entered the house, questioning why she would make up such a story. On impulse, he tried the phone and, to his amazement, got a dial tone. He punched in his brother Shane's cell-phone number. It was answered on the second ring.

"Lantry?" There was both relief and fear in Shane's voice.

"I'm okay."

"Is she holding a gun on you?"

"No, she's gone."

"Gone?"

"We went off the road yesterday and ended up spending the night in a ranch house. When I woke up this morning, she'd taken off on one of the horses." He hesitated. "She has the gun."

Shane swore again. "But you're all right?"

"Just fine," Lantry groused.

"She can't have gone far. Not as deep as the snow is," Shane said. "Where are you?"

He'd noticed the address on some old mail in the kitchen. "Apparently, I'm in Joe and Mabel Thompson's place south of town." Lantry didn't have a clue where that was. Or where Dede Chamberlain was right at this moment.

But he sure would have liked to get his hands on her.

DEDE RODE THROUGH THE snowdrifts, the horse sending the light snow into the cold air around them. She could see her breath, steam blowing from the horse's nostrils as the animal busted through the snow, the mountains rising from out of the horizon in the distance.

The blizzard had left the landscape looking like glistening white sensuous waves, the snow almost blinding once the sun came up. The land looked glazed smooth. There was nothing but white as far as the eye could see. It lay under a crystalline blue sky that was so intense it hurt to look at.

Dede had gulped at the sight of the huge horses and had been forced to tamp down her fear this morning before daylight.

"You can do this," she'd whispered to herself as she approached one of the horses.

She hadn't lied to Lantry last night when he'd asked her if she rode. She didn't. Not anymore.

As she slipped a halter onto the friendliest of the horses, the one who hadn't shied at her approach, she told herself that riding a horse again was nothing compared to what she'd already been through. This was the real lie.

She'd been deathly afraid of horses since an accident in her early twenties. Her horse had lost its footing on the side of a mountain and fallen. They'd both tumbled down the mountainside. While her injuries hadn't been life threatening, her horse hadn't been as lucky.

Just the barn scents had her shaking. "It's from the cold," she'd told herself as she'd swung up on the horse. The horse shuddered under her, and, for one terrified moment, Dede had thought he might buck her off.

She had thought she'd never get on another horse after her accident. This day, sitting astride this horse, reminded her of that other place, that other life and the pain. She was still terrified, and the horse sensed it, making it even more dangerous.

But danger was relative. The horse might throw her. Or take off and end up trampling her. The alternative, staying behind to go back to the hospital, was certain death. But try as she might, she couldn't relax and feared she had lost her original love of horses forever.

She slowed and glanced over her shoulder, half expecting to see Lantry coming after her on one of the other horses. Common sense told her that he was just glad to be rid of her. He hadn't believed her. That would be his worst and last mistake, she thought with no small regret.

If Frank had given his lawyer something for safekeeping, then maybe she could have helped save Frank, Lantry and herself. But if she was wrong about that, then she was wrong in thinking she could save any of them.

She told herself she had no choice. Lantry would be safer without her. In fact, leaving him was probably the best thing she could have done. Now she would be the focus of Ed and Claude's deadly hunt.

Dede stared at the mountains ahead of her. She had no real plan. Just reach the highway and take her chances getting a ride. Maybe not everyone had heard about the escapees. At least she wasn't still wearing a Santa costume. Thanks to the clothing Lantry had found for her, she was dressed like everyone else in the county now.

As she rode, the cold stinging her cheeks, she tried to convince herself that it was time she looked after Dede and quit worrying about everyone else.

But Lantry Corbett wasn't a man easily forgotten. Not the ruthless divorce lawyer—the cowboy who'd kissed her last night in front of the fire.

At a fence, she slid from the horse, relieved to get off the beast at least for a few moments. She opened the barbed-wire gate and, after walking her horse through, closed it again. That's when she saw the single set of pickup tracks and realized she'd reached a road.

As she debated which direction to head, she heard a sound. An instant later, a vehicle appeared from over a rise. As the rig bore down on her, Dede realized she had nowhere to run. She couldn't outrun the vehicle on horseback nor was there time to reopen the gate and take off across the pasture.

Better not to run anyway. Better to hope the driver just thought she was out for a ride and kept on going.

Sunlight glared off the windshield, obscuring driver and passenger as the SUV roared toward her.

She shielded her eyes from the glare as the driver hit the brakes, noticing the smashed front end as the SUV came to a stop just feet from her and the horse. Dede already had her story ready about her early morning ride when both doors of the SUV swung open.

She had only an instant before she was tackled to the ground, her head pushed deep into the snow as her wrists were bound behind her and she was dragged to the back of the SUV and tossed inside.

LANTRY STORMED AROUND THE ranch house, wearing a path between the fire and the front window. He'd made himself some breakfast, just to keep busy.

Too bad he couldn't corral his thoughts. They ran wild, rehashing every conversation he'd had with Dede Chamberlain, looking for other lies. He knew it was futile. The woman was sick. Deranged. How could he expect anything she said to make sense?

But it nagged at him anyway, driving him up the wall. He couldn't get Dede off his mind. Or how she'd fooled him. Or how he'd kissed her. He was still mentally kicking himself.

Shouldn't he have been able to spot deceit?

Except that he hadn't cared if his clients lied to him or not. It was all the same to him since with divorce it really didn't matter. It went without saying that there were two sides to every story. The only side he needed to know was his client's.

With that thought, he went to the phone, put in a call to the newspaper in Houston and asked a reporter to look for a story on a jewelry burglary. He recalled something about the case, but not enough to verify if Dede had been telling him the truth.

Lantry figured that if he could prove Dede had lied about that, then he could just assume all the rest of it was hogwash, as well.

"It would have been in late March or early April," he told the reporter. Right before Lantry left for Montana. "One of the necklaces was supposedly worth a million dollars."

"More like one point six million dollars," the reporter said. "Sure, I remember that story."

"Do you recall the name of the woman who was burglarized?"

"Give me just a minute." The reporter returned a few moments later. "Fallon. Dr. Eric and Tamara Fallon."

"Has the necklace been recovered?" Lantry asked, his heart in his throat.

"Nope. No arrests have been made, either, but a body was found in a canal last week that the police are saying might be Tamara Fallon. Some identification was found nearby. She and her husband were reportedly going through an ugly divorce. I understand he's been taken in for questioning several times, but no arrest has been made."

Lantry thanked the reporter and hung up as he heard the sound of vehicles coming up the road not long after the plow had gone through. Tammy Fallon dead. A woman from Frank's mysterious past. Add to that Ed and Claude, and what did you have?

Lantry shook his aching head. This all just kept getting crazier—and scarier, since at least some of Dede's story was true.

The first vehicle to arrive at the house was a wrecker, no doubt his brother's doing. The second vehicle was a sheriff's department SUV with his brother behind the wheel. The wrecker drove up the road and Shane and Lantry followed in the patrol SUV.

Lantry filled Shane in on everything Dede had told him while the wrecker operator worked to get the pickup out of the snowbank.

When he finished his story, he could see that his brother was as skeptical as he'd been. "I verified her story about the stolen necklace and the woman named Tamara Fallon. Apparently, Tamara Fallon's body was found floating in a canal last week. Her husband is a suspect, since they were in the middle of a divorce."

"This is all tenuous at best," Shane said. "Dede doesn't even know for sure that her ex-husband was involved in this burglary. She was also wrong about Frank giving you a gift. That should tell you something."

It told Lantry that they needed proof. "I should have asked her for the name of the private investigator she hired. Can't you at least see if you can find Frank Chamberlain? Do some digging into his past?"

Shane sighed. "I kind of have my hands full right now with three escaped mental patients on the loose and you to worry about. Looks like the wrecker's got your pickup out. Let's go see if it runs."

"Just a minute," Lantry said, grabbing his brother's coat sleeve to stop him. "What aren't you telling me?"

"Frank Chamberlain. He was found murdered."

Lantry couldn't hide his shock. "Then this proves—"

"Dede Chamberlain is wanted for questioning in his death. Frank was killed after she escaped the Texas mental hospital. The police have an eyewitness who places her in the neighborhood at the time the coroner estimates Frank's death."

"No way," Lantry said, shaking his head. He thought of Dede's face when she was talking about Frank, about her marriage. Those tears had been real, that pain and heartache genuine.

"She loved him. Still loves him after everything he did to her. There's no way she killed him."

"Frank was beaten with a lamp base. It has the earmarks of a crime of passion, and Dede's fingerprints were found on the lamp."

Lantry swore. "She lived in that house. Of course, her fingerprints—" He saw that he was wasting his time with this tack. "Won't you at least check into Frank Chamberlain's background? Find out if he really was involved with Tamara Fallon in the security business and if there were other burglaries as Dede says. Would you at least do that for me?"

"If you promise me you'll go straight to the ranch," Shane said. "The folks are worried sick about you. They won't be satisfied until they see for themselves that you're all right. And if you should hear from Dede—I hope I don't have to warn you how much trouble you'd be in if you help a woman who is not only wanted for questioning in her ex-husband's murder but an escapee with a growing criminal record."

"No," Lantry said with a brusque shake of his head. "You don't have to warn me."

"Get some sleep. You look like hell and you're cranky," his brother said as he squeezed Lantry's shoulder.

He knew how much he'd worried his family and his

brother—even more since Shane, the former Texas Ranger, knew just how dangerous these types of situations could be.

"So there hasn't been any word on Dede?" he asked, before getting out of the patrol car.

Shane shook his head. "We have law enforcement and border patrol looking for all three of them. If they're still in this part of the county, we'll find them."

That's what worried Lantry. It would be just like Dede to resist arrest. With everybody so worked up and her armed, she could get herself killed.

The irony wasn't lost on him. Dede was convinced that if she went back to the state hospital she'd be dead. Now she could be facing the death penalty for murder in Texas.

Lantry racked his brain as to what to do next as he drove back toward the Trails West Ranch. He couldn't just sit back and not look for Dede. She hadn't killed her husband. The eyewitness was mistaken. Or lying.

If Frank was involved in that burglary and that necklace was still missing, then wasn't it more likely that his buddies Ed and Claude had killed him?

A thought struck him.

At the top of a rise, Lantry stopped the pickup and reached for his cell phone. Good, he had service.

Dede had been so damned sure that Frank had given him something for safekeeping. What Lantry couldn't get past was that all her reasoning made sense. Frank would have trusted him. If the man really had something he wanted kept safe, why not give it to his lawyer?

Dede might have lied about riding a horse, but as he

hit the number on his speed dial, he thought of his wrecked Lamborghini. He couldn't discount everything she'd told him.

"WHAT A NICE SURPRISE," VIOLET said from behind the wheel of the SUV as she gunned the engine, shooting down the narrow track of road. "Been enjoying your stay in our pleasant little community?"

"Not particularly," Dede said from the backseat.

"Oh?" Violet was studying her in the rearview mirror. "Didn't find that man you were looking for? Corbett, wasn't that his name?"

Dede met Violet's crazy eyes in the mirror. How had Violet known that? Dede hadn't told her, and it was doubtful Violet could have heard through the White-horse grapevine.

She felt her pulse jump. Violet had been carrying two Santa suits the night they escaped, Roberta only one. Violet had been planning on taking a third person out with her and Roberta all along.

Dede had thought taking her along on the escape had been impulsive on Violet's part. Now she doubted that. Hadn't she been surprised how easy it had been for them to escape? She'd known it had to have been an inside job.

She'd just never considered Claude had been behind it. But Violet had known she was on her way to White-horse. Known she had been going there to talk to Lantry Corbett.

"A large man with gray hair and a scar was behind my escaping from the hospital here in Montana, wasn't he?" she asked now. "Calls himself Claude. Or at least he did. What else did he tell you?"

Violet met her gaze in the rearview mirror. "I don't know what you're talking about."

"Don't you?" Dede challenged. "Well, consider this. Everyone at the hospital will be under suspicion because of the escape. Claude really wouldn't want the truth coming out. So how do you think he plans to keep the three of us from telling on him, hmm?"

Violet's gaze narrowed. She shot a look at Roberta, who was also looking worried.

The only question that remained was why Claude would help her escape. Because he thought it would be easier to kill her outside the hospital? He knew she couldn't possibly have whatever he and Ed were looking for.

Her blood turned to ice. Was it possible they'd hoped she would lead them to Lantry Corbett—just as she'd done?

THE PHONE RANG TWICE, AND Lantry was starting to wonder if the office was closed for the rest of the week because of the Christmas holiday.

"Mr. Corbett's office."

Of course the office was open just days before Christmas. Divorce never took a day off—*especially* during the holidays, when there were always more domestic disputes than any other time.

"Shirley, it's Lantry."

"Merry Christmas," she said pleasantly. He could imagine his elderly secretarial assistant in her prim business suit sitting, back ramrod straight, behind her immaculate desk. "How is everything in Montana, or are you back in Texas?"

"I'm still in Montana." He told himself this was a fool's errand. "I need to ask a favor."

"Of course, Mr. Corbett."

"I need you to send me everything you have from the Frank Chamberlain case, anything he might have given me." He heard her hesitate and felt his pulse jump.

"Everything?" she asked uncertainly. "Does that include the large box he left for you?"

Lantry's heart pounded so hard he had trouble hearing, let alone breathing. "What box is that?"

"I was sure I mentioned it...."

"It's all right, Shirley. I'm sure you did. I just forgot." Or he hadn't been paying attention because the case was over and he couldn't have cared less about some gift Frank had given him.

Usually he told Shirley to open the boxes that were clearly gifts. If the box contained chocolates, he told her to keep them. Or share them around the office.

The booze found its way to the partners' lounge, since it was usually the really good stuff. Lantry never kept any of the gifts.

He was just thankful he hadn't told Shirley to get rid of the gift. "Would you mind opening the box?"

"I'd be happy to."

"It's not ticking, is it?" he asked belatedly, but Shirley was already off the phone. He could hear her in the background opening the box. He held his breath, suddenly afraid that the box didn't contain evidence—

but some form of detonation device. All the packages coming into the building were screened, but what if somehow this one had gotten in another way?

"Shirley? *Shirley!*"

Ed Ingram sat in the Great Northern Café sipping his coffee and listening to the group of local men talking at the table in the back. Regulars, from the way the waitress had greeted them as they came in.

The talk in Whitehorse was Violet Evans, one of the women who had escaped from the state mental hospital. Apparently, no one knew the other two.

From his table, Ed could see all the commotion at the sheriff's office. Cars had been coming and going all morning. He watched as a nondescript van with the state emblem on the side parked across the street.

Claude got out, looked both ways, then crossed the street toward the café. Ed noticed that Claude had put on a little weight, hadn't been taking care of himself like he should. A big man like that needed to watch his diet and get more exercise.

Ed turned his attention back to his coffee as Claude came in and took a seat at the counter close by, then turned on his stool to glance around the small space.

"Gonna be another cold one," Claude said in Ed's direction. "This normal weather for here?"

"Sorry, I'm just passing through on my way to Canada," Ed said.

"Canada, huh? I've never been up there," Claude said, getting up and coming over to the table. "I heard it's even colder up there. Are the roads open?"

"Last I heard, but there's another storm coming in tonight," Ed said. As his food arrived, he added, "Would you like to join me?"

"You don't mind? I do hate to eat alone." Claude took the chair across from him and glanced at the men in the back. One of them had been watching but turned back to the others, his interest spent.

Claude smiled, then turned his attention to the waitress, who'd just asked, "What can I get you?"

"Biscuits and gravy, two eggs sunny-side up and a side of bacon," Claude said.

Ed sprinkled berries over his oatmeal, watching Claude doctor his coffee with three packets of sugar and top it off with cream.

"What?" Claude asked quietly.

"Eating like that is going to kill you," Ed warned.

"Yeah? But what a way to go."

The locals wandered out, leaving the small café empty.

"Any news?" Claude asked after checking to make sure the waitress was in the kitchen out of earshot.

"According to the locals who were sitting in the back, so far no word."

"Nothing from your end?" Ed asked Claude.

"Just waitin'."

Ed knew Claude wasn't good at just waitin.' And it worried him. Claude made mistakes when he got antsy. They all did.

The waitress slid a huge plate of biscuits and gravy onto the table along with a plate of bacon and eggs. Claude unwrapped his silverware, tossed the napkin to the side and dove into the food.

Between bites, he said, "You got to hand it to Dede. She really is something else. I suppose you heard what she did over here at the jail." He chuckled. "Took the deputy's weapon and Corbett at gunpoint."

"Dede is much smarter than Frank ever gave her credit for," Ed agreed as he watched Claude devour the food as if he hadn't eaten in a week.

"You know she'll warn him."

"Yes, but how likely is he to believe her? The woman is clearly unbalanced. After all, she took him hostage at gunpoint." Ed shook his head. "I'm not worried about that."

"What if they don't catch her?"

Ed scoffed. "With every law-enforcement officer in Montana looking for them?" He grimaced as he watched Claude clean his plate, sopping up the last of the gravy with a chunk of biscuit.

"You eat like an animal," Ed said with distaste as he finished his oatmeal and blotted his lips with his neatly folded napkin.

Claude laughed. "I'm just a man with a good appetite." His cell phone rang. He dropped his fork to check it. His gaze shot up to Ed's as he took the call. "Claude here." He listened. "Uh-huh. Okay. Got it." He snapped off the phone and looked over at Ed. "Lantry Corbett's been found. Dede got away again. Looks like you're going to have to revise your plan."

Chapter Seven

"Mr. Corbett? It's a boat."

"What?" Lantry felt weak with relief.

"The box held a small wooden boat."

"The package was screened downstairs, right?"

"Of course," Shirley said. "The boat looks like a collector's item. Unless I miss my guess, it's homemade and quite old. Even...valuable, if you don't mind me saying it."

He smiled, his heart rate dropping a little. "Shirley, I need the boat and Chamberlain's file overnighted to me. It's important that you do it immediately. Would that be possible?"

"I will see to it myself. You know you can depend on me."

He had for years. "I know. Thank you. Also, let's keep this between the two of us."

"Confidentially as always."

Lantry realized that he'd offended her. "Shirley, have I ever thanked you for being such a loyal and competent assistant?"

"With a nice bonus every year, Mr. Corbett."

"But have I ever said it before?"

She sounded flustered. "Well, no, not exactly, but—"

"I'm sorry I haven't done that before now. I apologize. I don't know what I would have done without you."

"That is very kind of you. Is everything all right, Mr. Corbett?"

"Fine." He made a mental note to make sure Shirley was taken care of financially when she retired, which he guessed wasn't far off. He'd always dreaded that day. Now he realized she would retire only if he ever quit.

"I'll get that package off as soon as I hang up," Shirley said. "You want it sent to Trails West Ranch?"

"Yes. Thank you." The moment he disconnected the call, he punched in his brother Shane's number.

"Shane, I need you to call off the cavalry. Just give me some time to find Dede and—"

"Lantry—"

"I think she might be telling the truth. I just need you to—"

"Lantry! I've got news."

He braced himself for the worst—that the men after Dede had found her.

"The three escapees have been spotted," Shane said. "We just got a call from a rancher who saw them drive by."

"Three?" Dede was with the other two? How was that possible? "That can't be right. The rancher has to be wrong."

"I have to go," Shane said.

"You'll let me know when you find her."

"You aren't thinking about representing her, are you?

You're a divorce lawyer. She's going to need the best criminal lawyer money can buy."

Lantry didn't need to be told that. Frank Chamberlain had been a well-respected businessman who wielded a lot of power in Houston. Unless Lantry could prove that Dede's allegations about him were true and that she hadn't killed him... "Just let me know when you find her."

"I THINK YOU'RE JUST MAD ABOUT the last time we saw you," Violet said as she drove along the narrow, plowed road through the wintry landscape. "I see you finally got out of your costume. You must have done all right by yourself."

Dede said nothing, turning to look out at the drifted snow that swept to the horizon. She knew now that everything about her escape and getting dumped on the main street of Whitehorse had been choreographed, and not by Violet Evans.

Violet had stolen clothing for herself and Roberta, forcing Dede to remain in her Santa suit. No wonder she'd been picked up so quickly by the sheriff's department.

All part of the plan? She'd been manipulated, maybe from the beginning. From the moment Frank called her, begging for her help. Her heart ached at the thought that Frank had been in on this. She realized with a jolt that *Frank* was the one who told her about Lantry's car.

They already tried to kill my lawyer by rigging something on his sports car.

Tears of anger and hurt burned her eyes. Frank *could* have protected her *and* Lantry. All he had to do was give Ed and Claude what they wanted.

"I hope that necklace is worth it," she said under her breath. That's all it could be. Frank had helped with the burglary and somehow had gotten away with the million-dollar-plus necklace.

He'd doubled-crossed his cohorts, and now he must be hiding out while Ed and Claude came after her and Lantry. Had they hoped to use her and Lantry as leverage against Frank to make him come out of hiding?

Well, it wasn't working. And Lantry swore that Frank hadn't given him anything to keep for him.

"So did you find him and kill him?" Roberta asked.

"Who?" Dede had to ask since her mind had been on Frank.

"Corbett," Violet said. "Lantry Corbett. Your ex-husband's lawyer."

"No," Dede said, meeting the woman's gaze in the rearview mirror. "I only made things worse."

"I know what you mean," Roberta said. "Everyone's looking for us after what happened last night."

Dede felt herself start. She recalled how Violet said she was going to Whitehorse to make sure her mother never walked down the aisle. "What happened?"

"Shut up," Violet snapped. Her gaze in the rearview mirror wasn't aimed at Dede though—but to a spot on the seat next to her. "My mother got away last night, but she won't again. So stop nagging me. You hear me?"

Roberta made a circle with her finger next to her head when Violet wasn't looking. "Violet ran her mother off the road last night," she said. "Guess she's shaken up pretty good. Now her mother at least knows she's back in town."

"She'll know a lot more than that when I'm through with her," Violet said, glaring in the rearview mirror at the spot next to Dede. Roberta was watching her, looking a little worried.

"Where are we going?" Roberta asked.

"To hell," Violet said. "In the meantime, we're going to pay my mother another visit. But first we need to make a stop, and you, Texas, are going along for the ride in case we need your help. I'd say 'buckle up,' but I guess you can't, can you?"

Dede looked down from the hill they'd just topped to what appeared to be a ghost town. There were a few houses separated by empty, snow-filled lots. At least one of the houses was clearly abandoned.

Only one building had steam rising from it—a large barnlike place next to what could only be the one-room schoolhouse. Most of the playground equipment was buried in snow and looked as if it hadn't been used for a while.

Dede reminded herself that it was only days from Christmas. Of course the school would be closed.

"Welcome to Old Town Whitehorse," Violet said with the flurry of her hand as she pulled down a narrow road that had only recently been plowed, and stopped. "That is where I grew up."

"I thought you lived out of town," Roberta said.

"Just up the road."

Dede heard the irritation in Violet's voice and saw her frown at the other woman. She'd felt the tension between them the moment they'd abducted her from the mental hospital.

"See that building," Violet said, pointing at a large structure next to the schoolhouse. "That's the White-horse Community Center."

"I thought Whitehorse was to the north," Roberta piped in.

"This was the original Whitehorse. Then the railroad came through and everyone moved north to be next to it," Violet said, scowling at Roberta. "My family settled this land."

"Fascinating," Roberta said and yawned.

Violet seemed to clamp down on her temper, but Dede could tell it took a lot of effort. "We're going to wait until those people decorating for the wedding are finished, and then we are going down there to redecorate."

"That seems a little childish," Roberta pointed out. "I thought we were going to stop the wedding. That doesn't sound like it will do—"

"Shut up!" Violet screamed, making Dede jump. "Do you believe this bitch?" she asked, turning to look back at Dede. "This is *my* show. You're just along for the ride. So shut the hell up."

Roberta pouted, and the inside of the SUV fell silent. Dede didn't dare move for fear Violet would turn on her.

The vehicles that had been parked in front of the community center began to leave.

But Violet didn't move. She sat staring down at the town her ancestors had helped found. When she finally did start the SUV, she didn't head for Old Town White-horse, and Dede had a bad feeling that this might be the end of the ride for both herself *and* Roberta.

"Lantry!" Juanita was the first to see him when he walked into the main house at Trails West Ranch. As usual, there was something cooking in Juanita's big kitchen.

She clasped both of his hands. "I am so glad you're all right. We have been so worried."

"Thank you." He followed her down the hall to the large living room with huge windows that looked out over the ranch. He hadn't even stopped at his cabin, some distance from the main house, to clean up. He knew Shane had called the family and they were waiting for him.

They were. Everyone turned as he came in. His brothers Russell, Dalton and Jud and their wives, as well as his father and his father's wife, Kate. The relief he saw in their faces made him feel guilty for making them worry. He felt responsible for at least some of this, given his chosen profession—and how callous he'd been about his clients and their exes.

"I'm fine," he said to the crowd, his gaze settling on his father. Grayson smiled and nodded.

"We heard you'd been taken at gunpoint by a crazy woman," Kate said and rushed to hug him. "We were so worried."

"I'm fine, and Dede Chamberlain wouldn't have harmed me." His words surprised him in that he believed them to be true. Even as angry as she'd been at him.

"You'll join us for dinner, won't you?" Grayson asked. His father loved having his entire family at the ranch's large dining-room table. That's when he seemed the happiest.

But eating with his rambunctious family was the last thing Lantry could do right now. "Thank you, but I need to get a shower, a change of clothes and take care of some things."

"Of course," Grayson said amicably as he looped an arm around his son's shoulders. "You probably need some time alone to take all this in. Juanita will save you some dinner. It's just good to have you home."

Home. Lantry didn't think of Trails West Ranch or Montana as home. And yet he didn't think of his condo in Houston as home, either. The only place he'd ever really felt at home had been the family ranch in Texas. But Grayson had sold that after marrying Kate and moved lock, stock and barrel to Montana.

"I just wanted you all to see that I'm fine," he said, excusing himself. As he left, he heard his brothers horsing around and their wives trying to intercede. Everything was back to normal with the Corbetts.

All of them except me, he thought as he drove down to his cabin by the creek. His father had ordered a half-dozen cabins built for his sons for when they visited Montana.

Now, with three of them married, houses were in various stages of construction on the ranch, with everyone still living in the cabins spread out in a half-moon shape some distance from the main house.

Lantry knew that even when his brothers' houses were completed, they would spend most of their time at the main house. Just as Grayson had hoped. Just as the brothers' deceased mother had wanted and specified in a letter she'd written before dying.

That letter, and the five letters she'd left for each of her sons to be read on their wedding days, had come as such a shock that Lantry and the others had drawn straws to see which of them honored their mother's memory by marrying first.

Lantry had gone along with it just to keep peace in the family. His brothers knew he was never getting married, so it would come as no surprise when he reneged on the pact. He figured by that time the others would be married and too busy to care.

At his cabin, he stripped, showered and changed. Shane still hadn't called. Did that mean they hadn't found Dede and the others? If there had been a shooting, it would take his brother longer to call him.

Shane had told him to stay at the ranch, but he couldn't do that. Lantry grabbed his pickup keys. As he stepped out on the small cabin porch, he realized he'd left his cell phone inside and started to turn back when he heard the thwack of something striking the log next to his head. Bark and bits of wood flew into the air, several splinters embedding in his cheek.

He dove back into the house, but not before two more shots were fired—one hitting the door, another taking out the lamp on the table behind him. He slammed the door and belly-crawled over to his cell phone.

"Someone just tried to kill me," he said the moment his brother Shane answered.

VIOLET DROVE ONLY A SHORT WAY before she stopped again. The area looked desolate, but this whole country did. For miles there was nothing but snow, broken occasionally by a house or tree.

"You aren't going down there," Roberta said from the front passenger seat.

Dede looked to see what Roberta was referring to. An old farmhouse sat among some outbuildings in a gully nearby.

"I need to see my mother," Violet said in a strange, little-girl voice that made both Dede and Roberta look over at her in alarm. "I know she's down there."

"Your mother will call the cops, and we'll all be caught," Roberta said, getting angry. "I thought we were going to—"

Violet pulled the keys out of the ignition and opened her door. "You don't like it, take a hike," she said as she got out.

"That woman is crazy," Roberta said as Violet slammed the door and headed off down the hill toward the house where apparently she'd grown up.

Roberta slid down in her seat and closed her eyes as if planning to take a nap.

Dede saw her opportunity and began to work at freeing her hands. Violet had tied her with cotton rope that was now cutting off her circulation. With both her wrists bound, she had no chance of getting away from these two, and she hated to think what would happen if she stayed with them much longer.

She had to agree with Roberta. It was crazy, Violet going down there. No matter how it went, Dede worried it would go badly for Violet's mother. Or Violet.

And if Violet's mother called the cops, Dede and Roberta would be caught, as well.

"You know she talks to her grandmother who's been dead for years," Roberta said sleepily.

Dede knew Violet talked to someone who wasn't there. "She must have loved her grandmother."

Roberta laughed so hard the SUV shook as she sat up a little. "Her grandmother is the one she really wants to kill, but it's tough to kill someone who's already dead, you know? That old hag must have been a real piece of work. Violet's still scared of her."

Through the frost-rimmed window, Dede watched Violet approach the house. "What do you think her mother will do?"

Roberta shrugged. "What would you do if the daughter who'd tried to kill you came calling?"

Run like the devil, Dede thought.

Roberta seemed to realize that Dede was up to something. She glanced back at her.

"Could you untie me? This is really uncomfortable."

Roberta frowned. "I don't think so."

"We're all in this together."

"Not even close. I'm not sure how you ended up in the loony bin, but you're not one of us."

"Please. I'm not going anywhere."

"Uh-oh," Roberta said, turning her attention back to the farmhouse below them. "Did Violet just walk in the house?"

Violet was nowhere in sight, and Dede could make out movement behind the curtains. She listened for the sound of a gunshot, closing her eyes, wishing she was anywhere but here.

Lantry popped into her thoughts, bringing with him

the memory of the kiss. She'd made a mistake not staying with him and taking her chances.

Sure. By now she'd be locked up at the local jail or on her way back to the hospital.

No, as crazy as it seemed, she had a better chance with Violet and Roberta than she did with Lantry Corbett. But that didn't stop her from working at the rope binding her wrists.

"I THOUGHT I TOLD YOU TO STAY back at the cabin," Shane snapped at his brother as Lantry joined him on the small hill overlooking the cabin.

Lantry stared at the spot where the shooter had hunkered down. There were indentations in the snow where the marksman had used a tripod to steady his rifle.

"He settled in to wait for me to come out of the cabin," Lantry said more to himself than his brother. "So he knew I'd returned to the ranch."

"It's this damned local grapevine," Shane said angrily.

Lantry looked over at his brother. "This proves that Dede was telling the truth."

"Unless Dede is the one who took the potshots at you."

"Right. She just picked up a rifle somewhere."

"Are you sure there wasn't one at the farmhouse you broke into?" Shane asked and nodded as he saw Lantry's expression. "That's what I thought."

"It wasn't Dede. You said yourself she was seen with the other two escapees," Lantry pointed out, ignoring the fact that he hadn't believed that sighting.

"They were seen in this *area*. Her friends could have dropped her off and picked her up down the road."

Lantry shook his head.

"You've put your trust in a woman who seems pretty capable of taking care of herself."

"If she wasn't capable of taking care of herself, she'd be dead right now," Lantry snapped. "She had plenty of opportunities to kill me back at the farmhouse. She didn't."

"Yeah, well, consider this. How many killers use a tripod to steady the gun and then miss three times? If someone wanted to convince you that your life was in danger, they did one hell of a good job of it, didn't they?"

Lantry hated that Shane had a point. Even a hunter could have made that shot without any trouble given the short distance he'd set up from the cabin.

"Did you check on the things I told you about the Fallon robbery or Frank's old associates?" Lantry demanded.

Shane sighed. "Dr. Eric Fallon reported his wife missing four days ago—the same time Frank was murdered. Her body was found floating in a canal not far from where Frank and Dede lived. Texas is waiting on a positive ID from the crime lab. She was beaten beyond recognition—much like Frank. So not only is Dede's ex dead, but her ex's girlfriend. It looks really bad for Dede, Lantry. I think it's time for you to face the fact that this woman can't be saved. Not even by you."

He didn't give Lantry a chance to answer.

"I've got to go talk to the folks," Shane said. "I think the shooter made his point and won't be coming back, but just to be safe, keep your head down. Maybe you should move up to the main house."

"Sure, and put the family in the line of fire?" Lantry

shook his head. "I think the best thing I can do is get as far away from the ranch as possible."

"Don't be a damned fool. Just because you didn't get yourself killed this time doesn't mean that your life isn't in danger. This woman wants something from you. You'd best consider what will happen if she doesn't get it. Or, maybe worse, what happens if she does and no longer needs you."

Chapter Eight

Violet felt her heart lodge in her throat as she stepped into the house and saw her mother.

Arlene didn't move. Didn't speak. She just stood there, her eyes brimming with tears. And Violet knew that her mother had seen her coming. Had expected her.

Why hadn't she locked the door? Or gone to her fiancé's house to stay where she'd be safe?

Was her mother insane? Probably. Didn't it run in families, this mental-illness stuff she'd read so much about?

"I—I—" Violet's voice broke, and she felt her own eyes fill with tears.

"I was hoping to see you," Arlene said quickly. "It's been too long." Her mother was acting as if this was just a visit from her oldest daughter.

"You haven't seen me because you haven't come up to the hospital," Violet said, even though she knew that wasn't true.

"You always refused to see me," Arlene said quietly.

"I've been dealing with some things." She looked

around the house for a moment, her throat tight, that old pain in her chest making it hard to breathe. "You got rid of my room, my things…." She cleared her throat, the dam of hot tears breaking and rolling down her cheeks.

"I packed up all your things and put them in storage. I didn't think you'd ever want to come back to your room," Arlene said. "You can get them out anytime you want. I have a key for you."

"You've changed," Violet said, making a swipe at her tears and trying to steady herself. "You cut your long hair." Her mother had always worn her hair long and tightly pulled back from her face. Floyd, Violet's father, didn't believe in wasting money at the beauty shop. Neither did his mother, she thought bitterly, remembering arguing with her grandmother—and losing—for a salon cut.

Arlene touched the soft curls and looked embarrassed. "I've been trying to change."

"Obviously it's working. You're getting *married*." The unfairness of that formed a jealous, resentful bile in her stomach.

"You'd like Hank," Arlene said. "He's a good man."

This whole conversation had taken on a surreal feel, and Violet wondered if she'd only imagined it—until she heard her dead grandmother speak up from where she was sitting on the couch.

"Enough of this inane chitchat. Shoot her and get it over with," Grandma snapped.

Something in Violet snapped as well. She pulled the gun from the pocket of her coat and pointed it at her mother.

Arlene didn't react. If anything, she seemed calm, resigned.

"You didn't protect me from that old woman."

"She was your father's mother. I was young. I…" Arlene shook her head. "I have no excuse. I should have protected you from her. I didn't."

"Both of you are sniveling whiners," Grandma said from the couch. "I tried to give you some backbone. But you can't make a silk purse out of a sow's ear."

DEDE'S EYES FLEW OPEN AT THE sound of gunshots. Her stomach clenched with fear as Violet came racing out of the farmhouse on the hill below them, running through the snow, a gun clutched in her hand.

"I hate to say I told you so," Roberta said.

"I'm not sure that would be a good idea right now," Dede said tactfully, even though her heart was racing and she felt sick. "Violet seems a little upset."

A feeling of impending doom had settled like a rock in Dede's chest as she watched Violet fall in the snow just yards from the SUV. Gut-wrenching sobs were coming out of her as she got to her feet and stumbled the rest of the way to them.

Jerking open the driver's side door, Violet practically fell into the driver's seat. She was covered with snow but seemed oblivious to the cold as she stuffed the gun into her coat pocket and fumbled to insert the key into the ignition.

Dede, fearing more bloodshed, prayed that Roberta kept her mouth shut.

The moment the engine caught, Violet stomped on

the gas. The SUV fishtailed through the deep snow and back onto the road.

Violet glanced in the rearview mirror. But not at Dede. Then she just drove. For a mile or so no one spoke.

"So, did you kill her?" Roberta asked.

"Yes." Violet's voice sounded hoarse.

"Good," Roberta said. "Now you can get well."

Dede felt as if she might throw up. Violet looked over at her fellow inmate and actually smiled. "Yeah, maybe you're right." But when she glanced in the rearview mirror, Dede saw her haunted, lost look. Violet didn't believe it any more than Dede did.

"Have you ever been to Mexico?" Violet asked Roberta. "I've been thinking I'd like to go there."

"I like Mexican food," Roberta said. "In fact, I could use some right now."

"You can eat all the Mexican food you want once we get there," Violet said, sounding dreamy. "It's warm down there. We'll never have to wear a coat again. Imagine that."

Roberta had opened the glove box and pulled out a couple of candy bars. She was busy unwrapping one. Neither she nor Violet seemed to be paying attention to the road ahead.

Dede could see a stop sign ahead. They were coming to a four-way stop. Violet wasn't slowing down. She seemed lost, as if in a daydream on some warm, sunny Mexican beach.

Nor did either appear aware of the sheriff's department cruiser racing toward them from the left. Or the other from the right on the crossroad.

"Violet," Dede said, but it was too late. Violet didn't have time to react before one of the sheriff cars reached the intersection and skidded across the snowy road, blocking it. The second car came flying in, and suddenly Violet was standing on the brakes.

Dede tumbled to the backseat floorboard as the SUV skidded on the snowy road. All she saw from where she lay was snow flying through the air. There was a sudden thud that slammed her into the backseats as the SUV came to a stop.

The air seemed to suddenly fill with the wail of sirens as Dede let out the breath she'd been holding and red and blue lights rotated against the backdrop of the brilliant blue winter sky.

Before she could move, the SUV's doors were thrown open and she was hauled out with the others. She was finally untied, only to find herself in the back of a patrol car on her way to jail. Or, worse, back to the mental hospital.

"I DON'T UNDERSTAND WHY YOU didn't just kill Corbett when you had the chance," Claude said, sounding disgusted as he bit into a large piece of pizza.

"Do you have to eat that in here?" Ed demanded.

"Where would you like me to eat it? Outside?"

Ed would have preferred that. "You could have eaten before you came by my motel. As for Corbett, we need him alive, remember?"

Claude chewed for a few moments, then said, "But we don't even know for sure that Frank left it with the lawyer."

"Exactly. So we need to give him the incentive to

save himself and Dede. Corbett is more motivated if he thinks someone wants him dead. Get it?"

Claude looked up, and Ed could tell that he hadn't been listening. Ed couldn't hide his disgust and marveled how much he and Claude had changed since high school.

Ed had grown, matured, was now civilized. Claude, well, Claude had just gotten older. He was still unfocused, immature, impulsive, uncouth and a slob. Nor was he particularly bright.

Claude would always need someone to look after him. That someone would always be Ed.

Claude's cell phone rang. Ed watched him gobble the last of the pizza, then wipe his hands on his jeans before answering it.

He nodded a few times, grunted, then said, "Got it." As he snapped the cell phone shut, he said, "They got our girl."

LANTRY DROVE HIS TRUCK up to the county road to meet the UPS driver. He had to see for himself what Frank had given him. He prayed it would be proof to clear Dede, to keep them both safe—once he'd turned it over to his brother.

With relief he saw the UPS truck come barreling up the road.

"You got something for me?" Lantry asked as the truck came to a stop, half afraid there'd been a mistake. That the boat had been from another client.

"Sure do," the man said congenially. "You must be anxious if you are out here waiting for me."

"I thought I would save you the drive into the ranch. You've got enough bad roads to fight today."

The UPS driver began to hum along with the Christmas carol playing on Lantry's pickup radio. He'd left the truck running, the radio on and the window down a little so he could listen for any word on Dede. So far, nothing.

The driver got out to help Lantry carry two good-size boxes to the pickup, sliding them into the extended cab behind the seats.

"Some kind of crazy weather we're having, huh?" the man said. "I was wondering if I'd even be able to get out here today. Glad to see the road was plowed. Just hope the wind doesn't kick up and drift it in before I can finish my route."

Lantry was distracted by the larger box he knew must hold the boat. "Let's hope the roads stay open for a while," he said, thinking about Dede, worrying about where she was and what kind of trouble she might have gotten into.

The moment the delivery man left, Lantry pulled out his pocket knife to cut open the larger box. The Christmas carol on the radio ended and the announcer came on.

"The Sheriff's Department has informed us that all three escapees have been caught."

Lantry pocketed the knife and grabbed his cell phone, cursing under his breath. Shane hadn't called to tell him.

"I have to see Dede," he said the moment his brother answered. "You have to hold her there at the jail until I can get the paperwork to stop the mental hospital from—"

"It's too late," Shane broke in. "The van driver already picked them up to take them back to the state mental hospital. Dede will be evaluated to see if she is competent enough to face criminal charges."

Lantry cursed. "She was all right, though?" He heard his brother hesitate in answering just a little too long. His heart dropped. "What happened to her?"

"She's fine. They had her tied up in the back."

Lantry let out a curse. He tried to reassure himself that Dede would be safe—until she reached the hospital. "How long ago did the driver leave?"

"Look, I don't know what—"

"Shane, how long ago did they leave?"

His brother sighed. "About twenty minutes ago. But Lantry, you have no legal—"

Lantry hung up. The van driver wouldn't have that much of a lead, not with the roads being as bad as they were. If Lantry could reach the main road from where he was, he could cut off at least ten minutes, maybe more.

"ARLENE, YOU COULD HAVE BEEN killed." Hank Monroe paced her kitchen, his initial fear receding. Now he was just upset. "When I found your note—"

"I needed to see my daughter. I knew she would come back to the house. I would have told you, but I knew you wouldn't approve."

"Damn right. How could you take a chance like that?"

"She's my daughter."

He looked at this woman he'd fallen so madly in love with and couldn't decide whether to kiss her or wring her neck. "What am I going to do with you?"

She smiled through her tears. "Hold me."

He saw then that she was trembling and quickly pulled her into his arms. At least Arlene had called after Violet left. He was thankful for that. Because he would have had heart failure if the sheriff's department had called first. One of the other escapees, a woman named Dede Chamberlain, had told the deputies that she believed Violet had shot and killed her mother.

"Violet needs my help, Hank. She came to me because she needs me. You didn't see her, didn't hear her—" Her own voice broke.

"Arlene, she could have shot you instead of shooting up your couch."

"She and her grandmother used to sit on that couch, Hank. I would see the old woman clutching Violet's arm and whispering things in her ear. She blames me for not protecting her from her grandmother. I blame myself."

"Arlene," he said, holding her at arm's length to look into her eyes. "You told me about your mother-in-law. You were as much a victim of that woman as your daughter was."

"Still, I should have—"

"You have to stop this. It isn't helping Violet. What can I do?"

"We need to get her help, maybe a private hospital closer to Whitehorse so I can see her more." Arlene's eyes filled with tears. "Can we do that?"

He smiled. "Of course. I will make arrangements right away to have her moved to a private facility."

"Do you think they'll allow that after what she's done?"

"I might have to pull a few strings," Hank said. Maybe all those years with the secret undercover government agency might come in handy after all. They owed him, and he was about to call in one of those favors.

He cupped her face in his hands. "I love you, Arlene." He smiled and brushed a rough thumb pad over the tears on her cheek. "I've spent my life looking for someone like you. I just don't want to lose you."

"You aren't going to. A herd of buffalo couldn't keep me away from the community center Saturday. I can't wait to be your wife."

He kissed her, and she felt that wonderful stirring that she still found a miracle. That she was given a chance of love at this age was beyond remarkable, especially after the mess she'd made of her life. And Violet's.

"I love you, Hank Monroe, because you've never asked me to be someone I'm not."

THE HIGHWAY LOOKED LIKE A deserted wasteland. For miles, all Lantry could see was snow. Drifts had blown in across the road even since the plows had been through. Where there wasn't snow spines across the pavement, there was black ice.

The state driver wouldn't be able to make good time on the highway, which meant Lantry should be able to catch the van before it reached the mental hospital. That is, if he drove faster than he should.

He hadn't seen another vehicle, not another soul, since he'd left Whitehorse. A brisk breeze stirred the top of the drifts, sending snow showering over the pickup.

The day was clear but cold, the sky a brilliant blue and the sun too low on the horizon to do much more than warm the inside of the truck cab as he drove.

Anxious and upset with himself for his part in all this, he sped up. The rear tires lost traction, and he felt the pickup shift and slide on the ice. He hit a drift, got the truck under control again and slowed down.

His cell phone rang. It was his brother Shane. He had ignored the other three attempts Shane had made to reach him, not up for a lecture.

But worried now that Shane might have some news, he snapped open his phone. "Yeah?"

"Where are you?" his brother demanded. His tone was officious—the deputy sheriff, not the loving brother.

"I might have something that proves Dede was telling the truth. I have to get her out of that van so we can figure this out."

"You stop that van and you will be obstructing justice." Shane swore. "Once she's back at the hospital—"

"It will be too late. Damn it, Shane, I helped her husband do this to her. Did you check on Frank Chamberlain's past?"

"I made a couple of calls. I'm waiting to hear. That's why I need you to—"

Lantry cut him off. "I haven't had a chance to check what Frank left me for safekeeping. But if I'm right, it will prove why he had Dede put in the hospital—and why someone killed him. Not Dede. I have to go." He disconnected before his brother could argue further.

As Lantry topped the hill, he saw a vehicle in the ditch ahead. It wasn't until he drew nearer that he recognized the rig—the state mental-hospital van.

It sat at an angle in the snow-deep ditch, both front doors ajar. He felt his skin crawl, a sick lump in the pit of his stomach.

He touched his brakes and rolled to a spot on the

highway a dozen yards back from the van. He looked down the long, empty highway and saw nothing but snow and ice.

Slowly, he climbed out of the pickup, leaving the engine running, and made his way along the edge of the highway as he came alongside the van. The driver was slumped in his seat, his cell phone clutched in his hand, his shoulder holster empty and a pool of frozen blood around him.

Heart hammering, Lantry stepped off the edge of the plowed highway into the deep snow of the ditch to reach in. No pulse. He peered into the back of the van. Another body lay crumpled on the floor, eyes vacant, clearly dead.

Not Dede. But for just an instant...

Lantry tried to catch his breath as he moved along the side of the van and, cupping his hands, looked in the far back. Empty. Dede wasn't in the van. Neither was the other escapee, Violet Evans.

What had happened here?

Had the driver been shot before the van left the road? Or after? Lantry couldn't tell. But it appeared from the way the bodies lay that the driver and the dead escapee might have gotten into some kind of struggle. The metal mesh gate between the driver and the rear seats was hanging open.

Lantry cursed under his breath as he studied the footprints in the snow next to the van. His heart pounded. Two people had gotten out of the van alive: Dede and Violet.

But as he checked the footprints in the snow along the edge of the road, he found only one set.

He felt his insides buckle as he looked back at the van. The only place he hadn't looked was the far side of the vehicle. One of the escapees now had the weapon from the driver's empty holster. Which one?

And where was the other one?

Dede was desperate, but still he couldn't see her killing anyone. Not her ex-husband. Not the driver of the van.

What if you're wrong about that?

He shook his head. It had to have been Violet. Which meant...

His blood pumping wildly, he bounded down into the deep snow of the ditch and around the front of the van, expecting to find Dede lying dead in the snow.

He rounded the open passenger-side door of the van and stopped. No body. No blood trail in the snow.

The rush of relief forced him to bend down, hands on his knees, until his head quit spinning. This was his fault. If he'd only believed Dede. If he'd gained her trust she would never have left the farmhouse this morning.

If he hadn't been so damned cynical when it came to marriage, divorce—hell, women. She'd been right about that, too.

What now? Dede was gone. Out there somewhere. And with at least one killer on the loose.

He lifted his head, saw the lone set of footprints in the snow. He let his gaze follow the path the person had taken and realized that one of the passengers from the van had gone down the road. The other had climbed over the nearly buried barbed-wire fence and crossed the pasture.

He blinked. Why would…? He saw them. Horses in the distance. Dede was headed for the hills on horseback. Again.

VIOLET EVANS FELT LIKE A NEW person as she walked down the highway. Killing her dead grandmother had finally freed her and apparently changed her luck because, unless she was seeing things, there was a car coming up the highway. It was the first vehicle she'd seen on this deserted highway since she'd started walking a good half hour ago. The car slowed.

As the car came to a stop just feet from her, the passenger-side window whirred down. She stepped over and leaned in.

Violet had walked a good five miles down the road before a car had even come along on the snow-covered highway. By then she was freezing. Her hands and feet ached, and the air coming from inside the car felt so wonderfully warm that even if this guy was a serial killer, she was getting in.

"Need a lift?" the man asked unnecessarily.

Violet gave him her best smile. She knew she was no beauty. Far from it. She'd been told, though, that she was almost pretty when she smiled. The person who told her that had probably lied, but right now she would do just about anything for a ride.

"Car went off the road," she said, wondering if he'd seen the van back up the highway. Not likely. He must have come from the west and only connected with Highway 191 about a mile back.

Otherwise he would have seen the van, and if he'd

stopped to check, he would have found the bodies and he would be hightailing it for the cops—not stopping to pick up a hitchhiker.

"The roads are terrible," he agreed. "Where are you headed?"

Mexico, she thought. She'd had a year of Spanish in high school, and she figured she could pick up the language easy enough as smart as she was.

"What about your mother's wedding?"

She flinched at the sound of her grandmother's voice beside her, mortified to realize even emptying her gun into the woman hadn't exorcised her.

"Stay out of this, you old bat," she said in her mind. Still, this car proved that her luck had changed and Grandma would just have to get used to the new Violet.

"Billings," Violet said to the driver of the car. She'd noticed the plates on the man's car. They began with a three, which indicated the Billings area, a couple of hours to the south.

"Well, that seems to be the direction I'm headed," the man said. "Hop in."

Violet didn't wait for him to ask twice. She opened the door and got in, closing the door quickly. "It's cold out there." She whirred up her window and rubbed her hands together, glancing in the side mirror. No cars coming up the road.

She was anxious to get going, but he made no move to get the car rolling again.

"You sure you don't want to go back to Whitehorse?" the man asked. "It's closer."

"No, I already made arrangements to get my car

towed and my boyfriend is waiting for me down in Billings." She reached for her seat belt, thinking that must be what he was waiting for.

For the first time, she gave him a good look. Definitely not a local. He had a Southern accent and looked like someone passing through. Neatly dressed, he was short but solid, like someone who worked out and kept in good shape.

She recalled the plate number on the car and realized it must be a rental.

What in blazes was he doing on the Hi-Line, that no-man's part of Montana, in the dead of winter? Not that she cared enough to ask.

Slowly, too slowly, the man finally shifted the car into gear and started down the snow-packed highway.

Violet let out a sigh of relief and settled back for the ride, thinking about a new life in Mexico.

"You never finish anything you start," her grandmother said from the backseat. "You've always been like that. Make a mess of things and then leave it for someone else to clean up."

Violet hated the truth in her grandmother's words. She *had* made a mess of this. She hadn't exorcised the old crone, hadn't solved anything with her mother—who was still getting married—and now she was all alone and on the run.

"So you're just going to let your mother get married?"

Yeah, Violet thought. She was. She thought of her mother. Arlene *had* changed. Violet wanted to change, too.

Some days she didn't want to punish her mother, didn't have the energy. And wasn't it enough that her mother wouldn't have another sleep-filled night as long as her criminally insane daughter was on the loose? Wasn't that punishment enough?

"You just want to go to Mexico," Grandma said. "Stop making excuses."

"Well, one way or another, you're not going with me," she said under her breath.

"Sorry, did you say something?" the man asked. He was studying her. She prayed he wouldn't make her get out. Her hands and feet were only just starting to warm up. She couldn't face being out there in the cold again.

"Your accent. I was just trying to place it. Where in the south are you from?" Could the man drive any slower?

"Texas. I'm up here on business. In fact, I think you can help me. I'm looking for someone. Her name's Dede Chamberlain, and I have a feeling you know where she's gone off to."

Violet's dead grandmother was the only one who wasn't surprised when the man pulled the gun.

Chapter Nine

Lantry started to reach for his cell phone, then glanced back at the van, hesitating. There was nothing now that could be done for the driver of the van or the other escapee.

Who knew where Violet Evans was?

But if he made the call right now to his brother at the sheriff's department, he knew that Dede could be too easily tracked down. He had to find her first, get her to some place safe where they could open the box from Frank and figure this out.

Which meant he had to move fast. While there was little traffic because of the slick roads and the storm, he couldn't chance that someone would come along soon, discover the van, call it in.

He stared at the tracks in the snow. Deep shadows filled in the trail she'd left. He squinted in the direction the tracks led, seeing the path she'd taken. First to the horses, then clearly riding one of them bareback toward the foothills of the Little Rockies and the ponderosa pines.

It still grated at him that she'd lied about being able to ride—not that he didn't understand why she'd done it. He'd lied to her, as well—and to himself. He would have let Shane take her this morning if she hadn't taken off—and apparently they'd both known it.

There was really no debate. Both the driver and Roberta were dead. Dede was still alive. At least, he prayed she was.

He had to find her. She would be cold and wet. She'd have to find shelter. There were cabins up in the pines. That's where she would head—just long enough to warm up, rest…and then what?

She didn't know the area, didn't have anyone she could contact for help. She was alone and afraid. And he was the last person she would want to see.

Lantry busted his way through the snow back to his pickup and drove up the highway looking for a secondary road that would lead him to the cabins up in the mountains.

He took the first side road. It had been plowed sometime during the storm so the snow wasn't but a few inches deep. Still, Lantry had to buck a few drifts as he watched for Dede's tracks. She would have to cross this road to reach the shelter of the pines and eventually one of the cabins.

He hadn't gone far when he saw where she'd reached the road and rode up it. He followed the tracks into the foot-hills until they left the road. Pulling over, he glanced back toward the highway. He couldn't see the van from here.

Which meant whoever discovered the van wouldn't be able to see his pickup.

Getting out, he kept to the trees as he followed horse and rider up the mountain. Snowflakes floated in the cold mountain air, glittering in the sun like crystals.

The snowcapped pines groaned under the weight of their white burden. He busted through the deep snow, following her tracks, glad when he finally caught sight of a cabin through the pines.

He'd been betting Dede would have been so cold and tired that she would look for shelter in the first cabin she came to. Apparently she had, since the tracks snaked up the hillside toward the cabin.

Lantry felt his cell phone vibrate in his coat pocket. He didn't need to check. His brother had been trying to reach him ever since their last call. Had someone reported the van and the gruesome scene below?

He'd gone only a few yards farther when he smelled it. Smoke. Of course, Dede would have made a fire to warm up. She would have felt safe enough and been desperate to dry her clothing before she could go on.

As he followed the scent of wood smoke through the trees, he worried what kind of reception he would get when he found her.

"WHO THE HELL ARE YOU?" VIOLET asked the man holding the gun on her.

"You can call me Ed. I'm a friend of Dede's. So where is she?"

Any other time, Violet might have found this funny as she watched the man pull off in a plowed, wide spot next to a stand of ponderosa pines.

"How should I know where she is?"

"Because you were in the van with her back there," he snapped and thrust the gun at her. "You had to have seen where she went."

Violet had watched Dede wading through the deep snow as she crossed the pasture, thinking how stupid the woman was.

But Violet hadn't tried to stop her. She'd been more interested in saving her own neck. As far as she'd been concerned, Dede was on her own. They all were.

"What's it worth to you?" she asked the man with the gun.

He blinked in surprise. "What's it worth to *you?* If you don't start talking, I'm going to blow your brains out."

"I really doubt that," Violet said and brushed a lock of her straight, mousy-brown hair behind her ear. "In the first place, you don't want blood all over your rental car. In the second place, killing me won't help you find Dede. So what's it worth to you?"

The man looked furious, but he put the gun back in the shoulder holster and pulled out his wallet. "I've got two hundred dollars," he said, counting as he thumbed through the bills.

When she didn't say anything, he looked up, realization dawning in his eyes as he saw the gun. Apparently, he hadn't realized that whoever had shot those people back in the van might be armed. Or had he thought Dede had the gun—wherever she was? Clearly he didn't know Violet Evans, didn't have a clue whom he'd picked up beside the road, she thought. His mistake.

"Now," Violet said as she reached over and took the wallet from him. "I'll take that gun, as well. Lift it out carefully. I would really hate to have to shoot you and get blood all over this nice car—and keep in mind I'm one of the crazy ones."

He did as she told him, but she could tell she would have to make sure she never ran across this man again. Had she told him where she'd last seen Dede, she was sure he would have disposed of her at the next wide spot in the road.

The car engine was still running. She whirred down her side window and threw his gun out into the deep snow.

"Now put down your window."

He frowned but did it.

"Now get out," she said.

He hesitated, just as she knew he would. His second mistake.

The gun blast inside the car was deafening even with her side window down. His scream of pain lasted longer.

"Out," she ordered, waving the gun at him.

This time he didn't hesitate. She noticed with annoyance that his arm was bleeding all over the car as he fumbled to get the door open before stumbling out into the deep snow, falling and then staggering up again.

Violet put up her window, then slid over under the wheel. She slammed the driver's side door that he'd left open.

He was standing a few feet away in the snow, holding his upper arm where the bullet had grazed it. She whirred up the window, waved and drove off.

In her rearview mirror, she saw him scrambling to find his gun, and laughed, enjoying this more than she knew she should. Maybe she really was crazy. She shrugged. There was no way he could find the gun in time to stop her, so what did it hurt?

She was free. Again. Now she had a car and two hundred dollars in cash and some credit cards. Nothing could stop her.

"You know you have to go back to Whitehorse, don't you?" asked her grandmother from the backseat.

AS LANTRY NEARED THE CABIN, HE heard the snort of a horse and saw the thin trail of smoke rising from the chimney.

He slowed, reminding himself that Dede might be armed. Whoever had killed the van driver and Roberta had a gun—no doubt the driver's weapon.

Cautiously he followed the tracks in the snow around to the back of the cabin. The horse was tied with clothesline to a tree. Dede's footprints led to the backdoor.

Creeping up to the backdoor, Lantry listened for any sound inside. He was pretty sure he hadn't been spotted. Dede would have been watching the hillside, ready to run if she saw anyone. She would have taken the horse.

No sound came from inside the cabin. He noted the shattered glass where she'd broken the windowpane to gain entry. She was using some of his techniques, apparently.

He tried the knob. She hadn't bothered to lock the door. He pushed, and the door swung inward, creaking just enough that he knew he had to move fast.

He charged in, hoping to take her by surprise. But she must have heard him. She'd picked up the poker from beside the woodstove and now brandished it, making him glad it wasn't a gun.

"Take it easy," he said, holding up his hands in surrender. "I'm here to help you."

"Sure you are," she said, narrowing her gaze at him and tightening her hold on the poker. "Just like you helped me earlier?"

"I had nothing to do with you getting caught."

"And you wouldn't have turned me in first chance you got?"

"Why do you think I'm here? I heard from my brother that you'd been picked up and were on your way back to the hospital," he said as he took a step closer. "I couldn't let that happen."

He saw indecision cross her features and plunged on. "I called my secretary in Texas. I was wrong. Frank *did* leave me something."

Her eyes widened. He could see that she wanted to believe him, but she was afraid to. "You were so certain he hadn't, and now you find out he has?" she asked suspiciously. She took a step back at his approach, keeping the poker ready.

"Apparently he left it at my office after I came to Montana."

"Isn't that convenient."

Lantry supposed he couldn't blame her for not trusting him. "It's a small wooden boat, possibly a replica."

Her face crumbled. "He gave you the boat?" she asked in a whisper.

"You know about the boat?"

She looked up at him, a painful sadness in all that

blue. "I should. My grandfather made it when he was stationed in Panama during World War Two. He was a boatbuilder. He and *his* father before him." She lowered the poker, and he stepped to her, taking it from her.

She slumped against him for a moment before she stumbled back and sat down hard on a wooden bench by the woodstove.

There were a dozen questions he wanted to ask, but he knew they didn't have time for that now.

"Claude, the driver of the van…" Her voice broke. "He told me that Frank is dead."

Lantry nodded. "I'm sorry."

"They killed him because of me."

"No. They killed him because of whatever he was involved in. You couldn't have saved him. He was dead before you left Texas." He pulled her to him. "We have to get out of here."

She looked numb. "Tell me why I should trust you."

"Because I'm here. Now let's go."

ED DUG IN THE SNOW UNTIL HE found his gun, but by then his rental car was just a speck on the empty, snow-covered horizon.

He stood, breathing hard from the fury and the cold and the pain. His blood had left bright red splotches on the snow. His shirtsleeve was soaked, the blood freezing against his skin.

He looked up and down the long highway. Not another car in sight. He couldn't just stand here and wait.

In the first place, who was going to stop for a man

standing beside the road, coatless and bleeding, wearing a shoulder holster and holding a gun?

He tucked the gun into the shoulder holster and checked his wound. It hurt like hell, but the bullet had only creased the flesh. She hadn't hit the bone. He should be thankful for that.

Up the highway, he saw what looked like a building in the distance. He started walking, knowing he had to keep moving. The cold was already starting to settle. To keep warm, he thought of Violet Evans.

Just the thought of the woman made him burn with fury again. For the moment, Dede Chamberlain was forgotten. He would deal with her after he dealt with Violet Evans. Violet had made this personal. He would find her, and she would deeply regret what she'd done to him.

Ed hadn't gone far up the highway when he spotted a car coming toward him. He squinted against the bright sun reflecting off the fallen snow. The vehicle looked familiar. His heart skyrocketed.

He told himself he must be hallucinating from the pain. Why would Violet Evans be headed back toward Whitehorse when she'd been so anxious to go south?

Unless she'd come back to finish him off.

He smiled as he pulled the pistol from his holster. He didn't bother trying to hide. Where would he have hidden anyway? On both sides of the highway, there were high snowbanks from snow and ice thrown there from the plows. Beyond that was nothing but more cold white. Both lanes were glazed, as well.

He stood in the middle of her lane. Even if there had

been somewhere to hide and ambush her, he was sure she'd already seen him—just as he'd seen her.

He waited, the pistol ready as the car sped toward him.

FROM SNOW-COVERED SAGEBRUSH and scrub juniper to towering ponderosa pines, the land rose into the Little Rockies before falling as it dropped to the Missouri Breaks.

"Where are we going?" Dede asked, worried as Lantry turned onto the main highway and headed south. Back up the road toward Whitehorse, she could just make out the van in the ditch. She shivered and turned away.

"We're going to Landusky. It's a small town down the road. I know someone who has a cabin on the edge of town. We can stay there for the time being."

"Landusky," she repeated.

"It's an old mining town, has a great history. At one time it was as wild as any town there was. Smart men who wanted to keep breathing avoided Landusky, Montana."

He looked over at her when she said nothing. "I don't blame you for not feeling you can trust me. I thought a lot about the things you told me. When I talked to my secretary and found out Frank had sent me a present…"

"The boat." She shook her head. She couldn't believe Frank. "I wondered what he'd done with it."

The highway ahead ran straight south, snow piled deep on each side, the pines on the hillside laden in white. "I'm surprised it wasn't destroyed when your house was ransacked."

"I was so upset I didn't even notice that the boat wasn't there," she said. "Frank must have already gotten it out and hid it until he sent it to you. That means he'd been planning this for some time."

"You're that sure he hid something in the boat for safekeeping?"

"It has to be in the boat," she said. "If not, then you will go back to thinking I'm lying to you. Worse, that maybe I am as unstable as Frank led you to believe."

"You did lie about being able to ride a horse," he said after a few moments.

"I didn't lie. You asked if I rode. I said I didn't. Not anymore. I take it Frank never told you anything about me." She could only guess how Frank had portrayed her. "Never mind. I can imagine what he told you. I'm not originally from Houston. I was born and raised on a ranch in Wyoming."

Lantry tried to hide his surprise.

She smiled, anticipating his reaction. "I grew up drinking cowboy coffee and eating fresh-killed meat over an open campfire and riding horses." She took a breath and let it out slowly. "I had an accident on a horse before I left Wyoming. I hadn't gotten back on one until, well, not until this morning, when I had no choice. But if I never ride another horse, I'll be glad."

He didn't seem to know what to say. "What ranch?"

"The T Bar Double Deuce."

"I've heard of it. That's a big spread."

"I grew up hauling hay, slopping out barns and helping with branding and calving."

"So you've driven a four-wheel-drive truck in a blizzard before," he said, nodding.

"Just not in a blizzard like last night."

"You sound as if you liked ranching," he remarked with a look that said she continued to surprise him. "What made you leave?"

"I *loved* it. I would still be there if…" She looked up, hesitating. How much did she really want to tell him?

"Your horseback accident?"

"That was definitely part of it," she said noncommittally.

He nodded. "A man was involved, right?"

She smiled. "The first man I ever loved. My father. He sold the ranch after my accident."

"Oh. I thought—"

"I know what you thought."

He'd thought that her father was a ranch hand or maybe the ranch manager. Even when she'd said she had her own money, he hadn't really believed her. Just as it had never dawned on him that her father had owned the T Bar Double Deuce Ranch or that she'd been telling the truth about coming from money.

"I knew Frank let you believe I married him for his money." Her chuckle had a bite to it. "But I told you I had my own money. My father gave me my inheritance when he sold."

"I…" Lantry shook his head. "I'm sorry. I did have preconceived notions about you, apparently most of them wrong."

"Most?" she asked and felt his gaze go to her mouth. For a wild moment she thought he would lean over and kiss her—and run off the road.

"The road…" she said.

He turned back to his driving as the pickup got a little too close to the snowbank on the edge of the highway.

Lantry swerved, the rear end of the pickup fishtailing a little before righting itself. She heard him swear. She'd gotten to him, and what made it worse for him was that she knew it.

FARTHER SOUTH ON HIGHWAY 191, Ed stood on the snow-packed pavement, waiting. As the car rushed toward him, he raised the handgun and pointed it at the spot just behind the steering wheel. His finger brushed lightly over the trigger.

He was going to kill this crazy bitch. Blow her away and take his car back.

The roar of the engine carried across the Arctic landscape.

He would have only one chance. Fire the gun. Dive for cover.

Well, not exactly cover—just a frozen snowbank. And if he didn't clear the top of it, he could be caught between the hard-as-concrete bank and the grill of the car.

At the speed she was coming… He would just have to make sure he cleared the bank. Either way, Violet Evans was going down.

He took a breath, held it, finger resting on the trigger as the car bore down on him as seconds ticked off. He could smell the car's exhaust, feel the rush of cold air coming at him in front of the car.

He focused on the woman behind the wheel, counting off the seconds, the sight on the handgun aimed just inches below her chin. The gun would kick a little, just enough that the bullet should hit right between her eyes.

She was so close now that he could see the whites of her eyes. And then she did something so totally unexpected…

She swerved and hit her brakes, and he had an instant when he thought, *Hell, maybe she isn't as crazy as I thought.*

The car fishtailed and struck the unforgiving snowbank only feet from him, then pinged off to do a three-sixty in the middle of the snow-packed highway before smacking the opposite snowbank and bouncing off, disappearing behind him.

For a moment, Ed couldn't move. The car had come so close to him that he'd felt the back bumper brush his pant leg as it slid past. He began to shake as he realized how close she'd come to taking him out.

Had he moved a fraction of an inch, she would have gotten him. His skin went clammy, then ice cold as he realized that at this very moment she was probably putting the bead of her gun on his back.

He swung around, leading with the handgun in time to see the car come to a stop against the snowbank on the other side of the highway a good twenty yards away.

The car had come to a stop facing his direction, but unmoving. At least for the moment. He rushed toward it, gun aimed in the vicinity of where the driver should be, since he couldn't see her because of the angle of the sun reflecting off the windshield.

It wasn't until he came alongside and grabbed the door handle, that he saw Violet. Her head was tilted at an odd angle. He jerked open the door. Violet groaned and lifted her head. Apparently dazed, she stared stupidly at him, then made a grab for something on the passenger seat.

Before she could close her fingers over the weapon on the seat, he knocked her into next week.

Then he just stood there for a few moments, breathing hard. He was getting too old for this crap, he thought as he holstered his gun and reached across Violet for her pistol. Tucking the gun into his waistband, he considered what to do with her.

Leaving her beside the road was almost too tempting. But he doubted he could lift her up onto the high snowbank, and if he left her in the middle of the road, she would be found too quickly. Then the authorities would be able to put all their resources into finding Dede. He didn't want that.

With Claude dead, Ed didn't kid himself that he might not get the chance at Dede if she was picked up again and sent to the hospital. He had to find her. She was his bait to get what he needed from Lantry Corbett.

Ed looked up and down the highway. Someone was coming from the direction of Whitehorse, the vehicle still only a speck on the horizon. Hurriedly, he popped open the trunk and dragged Violet out of the car.

Violet was heavier than she looked. *Dead weight, so to speak,* Ed thought as he dragged her back to the trunk, thankful he'd gone for the full-sized car—and trunk.

He had to strain to pick her up. She tumbled in, banging her head. He started to slam the trunk lid, but realized he couldn't have her coming to and causing a ruckus.

He'd bought duct tape and a coil of rope in case he

needed it for dealing with Dede and the lawyer. He ripped off a length of duct tape, wrapping it around Violet's wrists behind her back, then taped her ankles, working quickly.

As he ripped off a strip to cover her mouth, he thought to check her pulse. Hell, he might be tying up a dead woman. Nope, she was still alive. He slapped the tape over her mouth and slammed the trunk lid.

As he started toward the open driver's side door, he saw that the vehicle was almost to him.

Hurriedly, he climbed behind the wheel and got the car going, glad the engine was still running. The solid ice snowbanks on each side of the highway had played hell with the body of the rental, but fortunately hadn't disabled the engine.

As the other vehicle grew closer, Ed saw that it was a pickup. He felt his pulse jump. It was the same color as the one Lantry Corbett had parked in front of his cabin.

In the rearview mirror, Ed saw the driver. Lantry Corbett. As the pickup passed him, Ed turned his face away but not before he'd seen the woman in the passenger seat. Dede Chamberlain. It seemed they were all on Highway 191 headed south.

Ed couldn't believe his luck. Lantry had taken the bait. Since he'd come from Whitehorse, he would have seen the van and the bodies inside it. But instead of taking Dede back to town and the authorities, he must be taking her some place where the two of them could be safe.

He watched the pickup keep going and continued at his slower speed, keeping the truck in sight as he followed at a safe distance.

Chapter Ten

Distractedly, Lantry glanced back at the car he'd just passed, then over at Dede. The woman just continued to surprise him—and worry him.

"Dede, I need to know what happened back at the van," he asked finally.

Her eyes filmed over for a moment. She took a deep breath and let it out. He listened without saying anything until she was finished. "That's pretty much what I figured."

He could feel her gaze. "You believe me?"

"Why shouldn't I?" he asked, glancing over at her as he drove.

Dede was studying him. "What changed your mind about me?"

What exactly *had* changed his mind? Not her angelic face. Or those innocent big blue eyes. Or the sweet taste of her when he'd kissed her back at the farmhouse. But he had to admit, some of that had played a part.

"I don't know. I wanted to believe you at some point. Then when I found out Frank had given me a gift just as you'd suspected and someone took a potshot at me…" He frowned. "You don't seem surprised."

"I told you Ed would try to kill you again."

"Except he didn't *try* to kill me. Unless he's a really bad shot, he purposely missed."

That seemed to surprise her. "You think he was just trying to scare you?"

Hell, he did scare me. "No, I think he wants something he thinks I have, and he just wanted to let me know he'll be coming for it."

"What Frank hid in the boat?"

Lantry nodded.

"And you have the boat with you?" she asked, glancing behind the seat into the extended cab and the two boxes there.

He found himself staring at her again. Only this time it had nothing to do with kissing her. "You know what's in the boat, don't you?"

"I told you—"

"I know what you told me. How about the truth?"

Those blue eyes narrowed into deadly daggers. "I am telling you the truth. I'm afraid the necklace is in the boat."

"From the burglary."

She nodded, then turned to look out her side window as the road climbed into the foothills of the Little Rockies.

He couldn't shake the feeling that she wasn't telling him everything. Was it possible that Frank had left something that might incriminate Dede Chamberlain, and that was why she'd risked everything to find it? Or that Dede had been after the necklace all along?

As he turned onto the road to Landusky, he checked

his rearview mirror. The large brown car they'd passed earlier was a dozen car lengths behind them, but no other vehicle was in sight.

Lantry tried to relax. They were safe. No one would think to look for them in Landusky.

"THIS IS WHERE WE'RE GOING?" Dede asked, both surprised and apprehensive as she spotted the handful of old buildings clinging precariously to the side of the mountain, half-buried in the deep snow.

"It's pretty much a ghost town now," Lantry said. "The town was named after Pike Landusky. He and another man discovered the gold here back in the late 1860s. Landusky was some character, I guess."

Lantry chuckled to himself. "As the story goes, one time he was taken captive by an Indian war party. Landusky, who should have been afraid for his life, attacked one of the braves—allegedly with a frying pan. The Indians, thinking he must be crazy, gave him two ponies to appease the demon and left him alone from then on."

"So what happened to him?" she asked, seeing how much Lantry was enjoying the story.

"Pike Landusky got on the wrong side of Kid Curry. The Curry brothers ranched about five miles to the south of here. Kid Curry killed him after an altercation in the local saloon. Landusky was buried nine feet deep—instead of six—to make sure he didn't come back."

Dede smiled, thinking Lantry would have fit into that Old West. She wondered, though, whether he would have been a Pike Landusky or a Kid Curry.

He drove through what was left of Landusky's wild town and took a side road that was even more narrow and lined with banks of snow. Then, shifting into four-wheel drive low, busted up through the pines on what appeared to be nothing more than a trail.

A large log structure appeared as they topped the hill. Lantry brought the pickup to a stop.

"We can stay here for a while," he said, cutting the engine. "It's all right. The place belongs to one of my brothers. He's having it built for his wife's birthday, but it's a surprise—so no one in the family knows about it except me. I took care of the legal work for him."

"This brother…"

"Not Shane, the deputy sheriff. Dalton, the cowboy rancher."

"How many brothers do you have?" Dede asked as they got out and waded through the snow to the backdoor.

Lantry fished the key out of its hiding place and opened the door. "There's five of us." He stepped in to turn on the lights, glad to see the electricity was still on. "It's kind of a mess because it's still under construction."

There were ladders and sawhorses, piles of lumber and tools, as well as sawdust and drop cloths.

"I guess I didn't realize your whole family had moved to Montana," Dede said, working her way through to the living room.

"It's a long story. Maybe I'll tell you about it some time." Lantry looked around. "The fireplace is finished, and at least one bedroom." He pointed to the loft. Apparently the interior decorator had finished up there, since she could see a large bed with a brocade spread and other furnishings.

"See if there's anything to eat in the kitchen," Lantry said. "I'll get the boxes out of the truck."

Dede wandered into the kitchen. Unlike the ranchhouse they'd broken into, these cupboards were practically bare. But she found some food in the refrigerator that the construction workers must have left.

As she walked through the beautiful log lodge, she envied Dalton Corbett's wife. To have a man love you so much that he planned such a wonderful surprise…

Dede caught movement out of the corner of her eye. Through the dusty window, she saw Lantry standing outside by his pickup. He was on his cell phone.

Her heart dropped.

"WHERE THE HELL ARE YOU?" SHANE demanded the instant he answered.

Lantry had stepped outside so Dede couldn't see or hear him use the cell phone. He knew he'd be able to get service because the town of Landusky was just down the mountain side. He had thought about telling her he planned to call his brother, but he feared it might make her run again. "We need to talk."

"What the hell is going on?" Shane asked, lowering his voice.

"I have Dede Chamberlain."

"When are you bringing her in?"

"I'm not." He waited until his brother quit swearing. "At least not for twenty-four hours."

"Twenty-four hours?"

"There's something I need to check out first."

Shane bit off each word into the phone. "Do you have any idea the spot you've put me in?"

"I'm sorry, but like I told you, I believe her."

"Damn it, Lantry, Dede Chamberlain isn't just wanted for escaping a mental hospital or two. Bodies are piling up. Frank Chamberlain, Tamara Fallon, the hospital guard, one of the patients…" A beat, then, "I'm waiting for you to sound surprised, damn it."

"She didn't kill anyone."

"And you know that *how?*"

"She loved Frank Chamberlain. She still does. And as for the guard and the patient, Dede told me that the guard stopped the van and told her to get out. He was going to kill her, Shane."

"The guard from the hospital? So you're telling me it was self-defense."

"Yes, only Dede never touched the guard's gun. If you check, you'll find that the guard is from Texas. He's an old friend of Frank Chamberlain's, Dede's ex, and he only recently got the job at the hospital up here."

"And what did she tell you happened after the driver told her to get out of the van?" Shane asked.

Lantry could hear the skepticism in his voice. Why did his brother always have to be a cop? "The other escapees saw what was going to happen. The guard opened the metal mesh door between him and them and Roberta went for the gun. She and the guard were shot in the scuffle. Violet ended up with the gun. Dede feared she'd be next and took off across the pasture and hid until she saw Violet hitchhiking up the road."

"At least that's Dede's story." Shane slammed a file cabinet drawer or something that sounded a lot like one. The noise reverberated through the phone. "Listen to me. You have to turn her over now, Lantry. Otherwise, you are looking at aiding and abetting. I don't think I have to tell you what kind of sentence that carries with it, since you're a damned lawyer."

"I need twenty-four hours. That's all I'm asking. By then I hope to have the proof I need and can file papers to keep Dede from going back to that hospital." He could hear his brother breathing hard on the other end of the line. "Shane, I know this woman didn't kill anyone."

"You don't know. You can't know her after spending only a few hours with her."

"Either way, I take full responsibility for what I'm doing."

Shane's chuckle held no humor. "Even you may not be able to use that high-priced law degree to get out of this one, Lantry. There is a state manhunt on now for Dede and Violet. Turn her over to me, and then you can work your legal magic to get her freed. In the meantime, I will do everything I can to help her."

"I know you would," Lantry said. "But I can't trust that the men after her won't get to her through one of the mental-hospital guards or some rogue deputy."

"You're talking just as crazy as she is," Shane snapped.

"Don't forget that someone took a potshot at me. Did either of the three escapees or the hospital guard have a high-powered rifle on them when you found them? I didn't think so. There's still a killer out there.

Give me twenty-four hours to find out why this person wants Dede and me dead."

"Do you believe this woman because of that face of hers or those big blue eyes or because she's actually telling the truth?"

"You should know me better than that," Lantry snapped back. "Check out Claude, the driver of the mental hospital van. He has a friend named Ed. That's all I know. But I figure Ed can't be far behind him."

"When I find you, I'm going to kick your butt all the way back to Texas," Shane said.

"Twenty-four hours." He snapped the phone shut and swore. He hoped the sheriff's department couldn't trace the call. He doubted it.

His brother was right about one thing: Dede had gotten under his skin. He just hoped to hell it wasn't for the reason that Shane thought.

SHANE HUNG UP, FURIOUS WITH his brother and yet more worried than angry. Lantry had no idea what he was dealing with.

He thought about Dede Chamberlain and could understand how someone could be taken in by her. But *Lantry?* The divorce lawyer had never even had a serious relationship. He dated but seldom, and he'd made it clear he'd never planned to marry. That was a given, but he'd also never gotten close enough to a woman to give a real relationship a fighting chance.

So what was different about Dede?

She was a woman in trouble. That alone was a siren call for any of the Corbett brothers, Shane thought with a groan. But sticking your neck out to save a woman was one thing. Lantry had crossed a line with this one.

Shane knew what had him so upset. It wasn't that every law officer in several counties was looking for Dede Chamberlain or even that she was wanted for questioning in three murders.

It was Lantry trusting this woman with his life.

Sheriff Carter Jackson looked up as Shane stepped into his office. They'd just come off a shift change, though Shane had no thought of going home. He had to find his brother before it was too late.

"I just spoke with Lantry," Shane said, shutting the door behind him.

"Okay," Carter said. "Let's hear it."

"Lantry found Dede Chamberlain. He has her."

"He's bringing her in, right?"

"He wants twenty-four hours. He says he's following some lead and will bring her in then."

The sheriff was shaking his head. "He needs to bring her in now. I assume you told him that. He knows about the murders?"

"He found the van."

"So those were his footprints we discovered." The sheriff let out a curse. "You said he's a lawyer, so he knows that he's now wanted for questioning along with aiding and abetting?"

Shane nodded solemnly. "I tried to talk some sense into him, but he's convinced that if he brings Dede in, she won't live long enough to make it back to the state hospital. Given what happened to the van driver and the other patient…"

"You know we can keep her safe here at the jail."

"I'm sorry, Sheriff, but, truthfully, I don't know that. Look what happened before. Don't get me wrong. I did everything I could to convince my brother to bring her in. But just between you and me, she might be safer with Lantry right now."

"But is your brother safe?" He shook his head. "Do you have any idea where he has taken her?"

"He can't take her to the ranch, because he knows I would arrest them both. I really don't know where he's gone, but I intend to find him." Hopefully before anything bad happened to him.

VIOLET CAME TO IN THE DARK. Her eyes flew open, panic making her jerk and hit her head. She let out a frightened moan and for a moment thought she was a little girl again and that her grandmother had locked her in the old coal bin.

She shivered at the memory. The cobwebs and spiders. The smell of sour earth. The sound of mice chewing somewhere in the dank basement. She had fought so hard not to cry. To cry meant her grandmother would leave her in there longer.

Violet quickly quieted herself as she realized she wasn't in the old coal bin, and her grandmother was dead—if not gone.

She could hear the hum of the tires on the highway over the roar of the big car's engine, and she could smell the too-sweet scent of recently cleaned rental-car carpeting where she lay.

Still, it took her a few minutes before she could

chase away thoughts of the coal bin. She rubbed her face into the carpet until it hurt, until she could no longer imagine the brush of cobwebs on her skin or hear the creak of her grandmother's shoe soles on the other side of the darkness.

As Violet slowed her mind to catch her erratic thoughts, she knew two things. She was still alive, apparently none the worse for wear except for a splitting headache, and she hadn't been dumped beside the road. Instead, he'd left her alive—and taken her with him in the trunk.

What worried her was why.

Had she been in his position, she would have made sure Violet Evans had breathed her last breath. But then, he didn't know her, did he, she thought with what passed for a smile beneath the duct tape.

Violet began to make plans for her escape. The first step was getting the duct tape off her wrists. That was made more difficult since her wrists were taped behind her back.

She felt around in the trunk, only to discover it was empty. What tools there were must be in some hidden compartment—probably underneath her. She searched the interior of the trunk with her cold fingers, finding rope and more duct tape. Definitely not a good sign. She kept searching until she found a rough spot on the metal frame of the trunk.

Meticulously she began to work at the duct tape, letting her mind drift.

Ed had made a mistake keeping her alive. One he would live to regret.

DEDE WAS WAITING FOR HIM WHEN Lantry came back into the house with the two boxes from the pickup.

When she'd seen him on his cell phone, she'd thought about taking off again, but soon it would be dark and the snow was even deeper up here in the mountains. The days up here, so close to the Canadian border, were short, and she was exhausted both mentally and physically, a part of her ready to concede. And yet another part of her was so angry and disappointed in Lantry that she wanted to stay and fight.

"Guess what," Lantry said as he closed the door behind him and set down the two boxes he'd brought in.

"I'm going back to jail. What a surprise since I saw you making the call."

His face clouded. "I *did* call Shane, but not to turn you in. I asked him to give me twenty-four hours. I didn't tell him where we are, and I sure as hell didn't sell you out."

Had she misjudged him again? "I thought—"

"I know what you thought. When are you going to start trusting me?"

"Maybe when you start trusting me," she snapped back.

"Damn it, Dede," he said closing his fingers over her upper arm and dragging her closer. "I've gone out on a limb for you." He shook his head. "By now there's an APB out on me as well as you. What more can I do to prove that I'm in this with you?"

He kissed her hard on the mouth, a punishing kiss that took her breath away. Then he practically flung her away from him, swearing under his breath.

"I'm sorry," he said as he dragged off his Stetson. "I shouldn't have done that."

The kiss was all her idea this time. Not that she gave it any thought before she went up on tiptoes and pressed her mouth to his. Just like the first time, his mustache tickled, but only for an instant before he dragged her to him, encircling her with his strong arms.

Her lips parted, opening for him, and she felt the tip of his tongue sweep over her lower lip. It had been so long since she'd felt desire, felt it run like a fire through her veins, felt it blaze across her skin.

She would have been shocked had she thought about how badly she wanted this man, but at that moment all reason had left her. Her body ached with a need for this cowboy, and Dede threw all caution to the wind as he swept her up and carried her to the loft.

He took her to the bed and set her down to look into her eyes. "Dede?"

She knew what he was asking. Reaching down, she grabbed the hem of the sweater he'd taken for her at the Thompson's ranchhouse and pulled it over her head, baring her breasts.

Lantry groaned and pulled her to him, his kiss as hot as her blood. She breathed in the scent of him as his hands cupped her behind.

She wrapped her arms around his neck and pulled him down with her onto the cool fabric of the comforter. Her fingers worked at the snaps on his Western shirt, needing to feel his flesh against her own.

He wriggled out of his shirt, tossing it aside, his mouth coming back to hers. She felt his warm palm cup her breast; the rough pad of his thumb brushed the hard nub of her nipple, making her arch against him.

"Lantry," she cried on a breath, her fingers going to the buttons on her jeans, then to his, both of them needing and wanting this human touch.

She couldn't hold back the satisfied sound that came from her lips when they'd finally shed all their clothing and he took her in his arms. She touched his face and looked into his dark blue eyes, seeing her own desire reflected there as he made love to her.

The first time was fast and furious, both of them breathing hard, holding tight to each other.

LANTRY LAY SPENT ON THE strange bed, the naked, warm Dede in his arms. As he stared up at the ceiling, a smile on his lips, he tried to remember another time in his life when he'd felt like this. Never.

That alone should have scared the hell out of him. But he wasn't a man who scared easily. He'd ridden wild horses, wrestled his fair share of steers to the ground and even rode mean bulls. He'd known his share of women, drunk his share of good wine and even better booze, and had more than his share of successes in life.

But he'd never known such euphoria as he did at this moment. Or such peace. He pulled Dede a little closer, loving the feel of her skin on his own, breathing in the musky scent of the two of them entwined.

He felt her stir, her breath tickling his neck. "You asked how all the Corbetts ended up in Montana," he said quietly. "You still want to hear?"

She nodded and snuggled closer.

"Our mother died when we were young. Dad's recently remarried. That's how we all ended up in Montana. His wife, Kate, was from here. Trails West Ranch was her family's. My mother was born on the ranch. Her father was the ranch manager." He shrugged. "None of us planned to stay here, but then Dad found some letters my mom left. She wanted us to marry Montana girls. Mostly Dad wanted us close by. One of my brothers came up with this inane idea that we should make a marriage pact. Russell suggested drawing straws to see who would get married first."

Dede started laughing. "You would never have agreed to such a thing. Not you. Don't tell me that you—"

"I drew a damned straw just to shut them all up." The truth was, he'd gotten caught up in the moment, wanting to do this for their mother.

"And now all but you are married or engaged?" Dede asked in disbelief.

"I'm not sure how it happened. I guess it made us all more open to marriage." He realized Dede was staring at him.

"Except for you," she said, daring him to disagree.

"I still think marriage is a gamble," he said, cupping her cheek in his large palm. "I've never even been tempted. Never met a woman who made me want to risk it." He looked into her big blue eyes. But then, he'd never met anyone like Dede Chamberlain, had he? "Until—"

She pulled away, drawing the sheet around her as she got out of bed. "Don't, Lantry," she said, her back to him.

"Don't tell you how I'm feeling?"

"No." She turned to scowl at him. "I don't trust your feelings. Not right now. It's too soon." She glanced toward the living room. "We don't know what's in that box down there, and I think we're both afraid to look."

He wanted to pour his heart out to her, but he knew she was right. And for a while he'd forgotten that she was still in love with her ex-husband.

Also there was that damned box with the boat in it— and whatever might or might not be inside.

Even if there was no explosive device inside that boat, Lantry wasn't fool enough to think that whatever was in there couldn't blow up. He and Dede might never make this mess right again.

Dede looked as worried as he felt. Still, he couldn't help the way he felt about her. He didn't want this to end, damn it. And he was scared that whatever was in that box was going to destroy the two of them.

"If we survive this—"

"*When* we survive this," he said, grabbing hold of the edge of the sheet and jerking it to free her wonderful naked body. He reached for her hand and pulled her back into bed, back to him, and then he made love to her slowly, deliberately, passionately as snow began to fall outside and the light began to fade to black.

It wasn't until later, when they lay in the bed listening to the snow pelting the window, that Lantry knew they couldn't put it off any longer.

It was time to find out what the hell Frank Chamberlain had put into that boat. Something so valuable that it had cost him his life and, just having it, could cost them theirs, as well.

Chapter Eleven

Lantry kissed Dede on the top of the head. Then, releasing her, he swung his legs over the side of the bed and dressed.

He could see the cold darkness of the evening through the curtainless windows downstairs. Earlier, when he'd gone out to call his brother, he'd heard a car go by. He'd waited to make sure it hadn't stopped. It hadn't.

Now he felt exposed. This is what it felt like being on the run.

Downstairs, he moved the two boxes into the living room, then built a fire in the fireplace with the scrap wood lying around.

Once the fire caught, he turned to the boxes, praying that whatever Frank had hidden in the boat would help them out of this mess.

He didn't even want to think about the laws the two of them had broken or the trouble they were in. The only way out was to find out the truth, expose the men involved and put an end to this. Then he would deal with the legal problems they would be facing.

At least if he could prove the danger Dede had been in, he believed he could clear her. That was his main concern as he pulled the box over in front of the fire-place and stopped to listen.

He could hear Dede in the shower. As he listened closer, he heard her singing. He got up and walked down the hall to stand outside the bathroom door. She had a beautiful voice. He remembered something. A photograph that had fallen out of Frank's wallet during one of their meetings about the divorce proceedings.

Lantry had picked it up from the floor where it had dropped and handed it back to Frank, who'd seemed flustered. But not before he'd seen the woman in the snapshot. She'd been playing a guitar and singing. Lantry had only gotten a glimpse of her. A young woman, college-aged, with long reddish-blond hair and big blue eyes.

With a jolt, he realized the photograph had been of Dede. What made his heart ache was the realization that Frank Chamberlain had hung on to a photo of the woman he was divorcing. Frank had never stopped loving Dede.

And Dede had never stopped loving him.

Stepping away from the door, Lantry went back to the box waiting for him. The present Frank had given him. Now more than ever, Lantry wanted to know what was inside. Taking out his pocket knife, he began to open the box.

He heard the shower shut off, the singing stop. He pulled back the cardboard flaps.

As he removed the packing material on top, Lantry

was taken aback by the sight of what appeared to be a small replica of a wooden boat from the 1930s or 1940s.

It lay in a nest of packing material, the mahogany wood lightly varnished and glowing warmly. The boat was perfect in every detail.

Looking up, he saw Dede come into the room. She stopped and hugged herself as she watched him lift out the boat.

"It's beautiful," he said in awe as he ran his fingers along the smoothly lacquered mahogany.

Dede nodded but said nothing.

Lantry held the boat up to the light. As he did, he heard something shift inside the hull. He felt his heart kick up a beat.

He glanced at Dede. Her eyes had filled with tears. Frank had let her down in so many ways. Would he let her down even more when they discovered what was inside the boat?

But as he inspected the boat, he could find no way to open it to get inside. "Dede, is there a secret compartment or door to get inside the hull?"

She seemed to hesitate, then came over and knelt down on the floor next to him. Her fingers trembled as she touched the slick surface of the boat, running her fingertips along the gunnels. She brushed over one of the tiny cleats, and a side panel in the boat popped open to reveal a compartment inside.

Lantry heard her let out a small sigh as she drew back her hand and looked over at him. He could almost see her hold her breath as he reached inside to work out a small padded bundle the size of his fist.

Glancing at Dede, he took a breath, then carefully began to unwrap it. Just as he'd feared. A nest of diamonds and gold appeared.

As he picked up one end, the diamond necklace unwound itself to snake downward in a long, glittering rope.

"So that was it," Dede said as their gazes met. "A simple case of greed." She stood, dusting off her pants as she went to warm herself in front of the fire. "I guess that explains why Ed and Claude are after us. Just as I feared. Frank double-crossed them and involved us."

It certainly looked that way. He could see that Dede was upset. Like him, she'd been hoping Frank had left a letter or document explaining what he'd done to her and why. Something that could be used to free her from the mental hospital, free her from Frank and the past.

Instead, all Frank had left was proof of his involvement in the Fallon burglary.

This explained what Ed and Claude were after. It didn't seem enough. Frank had lost his life for this. How could he have divorced and committed his wife for something this cold to the touch? That didn't jibe with the photograph Frank had kept in his wallet and Lantry's belief that the man had loved his wife.

While the necklace proved that Frank was involved in the burglary of the home of Dr. Eric and Tamara Fallon, it provided no insight into why Frank had given up everything for this. He'd been a wealthy man. What was another million or so dollars?

Apparently enough that, like Dede said, he'd

double-crossed his partners in crime and ultimately lost everything.

Lantry started to put down the necklace, sickened by the thought of what Frank had done, when the stones caught the light of the fire. He froze.

ED HAD PARKED DOWN THE ROAD IN a wide spot that had been plowed for snowmobile trailers. He could see where the trucks and trailers had parked, where the snowmobiles had been unloaded and run through the woods, where the riders had shared a few beers and some smokes before leaving.

The parking area was empty now except for a few cigarette butts and a six-pack of crushed beer cans.

Ed had settled in to wait for darkness, dozing off for a while to wake to the gunmetal-gray sky. He knew at once that something had awakened him and looked around, thinking it was a snowmobiler.

The car moved, and he remembered with a start that he still had Violet Evans locked in his trunk.

He got out of the car and stepped back to the trunk, standing in the growing darkness of the winter night. The sky reflected the steel blue onto the snow, casting the snow-covered land in an eerie light.

As he stood outside his frost-coated rental car, Ed had never felt more alone—even with Violet just inches away in the trunk. Frank was gone. So was Claude. The thought wrenched at his heart. Frank had gotten what he deserved, but not Claude.

Emptiness and loneliness filled him, amplified by the desolate frozen landscape.

One clear thought worked its way through his grief. He should have killed Violet. He couldn't remember now why he'd kept her alive. The vehicle coming up the road. That's why he hadn't taken the time to end it right there in the middle of the highway. He'd always planned on disposing of her body. He just wished that he had killed her when he'd had the chance earlier rather than wait.

The cold made his movements slow and clumsy, his mind seemingly just as sluggish. He shuddered from the cold, stirring himself into action. Finish this.

In the pale cold light he bent down and inserted the key into the trunk lock, then listened. Violet hadn't moved for some time now. No sound emerged from inside. Maybe she'd done him a favor and succumbed to asphyxiation.

He hadn't even thought about whether there was enough air in the trunk for her. With the tape across her mouth…

He turned the key. The trunk lid yawned open, and he had to squint, leaning in to see her in the tomblike, shadow-filled hole.

The blow took him completely by surprise. She seemed to spring out, leaping at him, the thick roll of duct tape catching the eerie winter light before it connected with his skull, stunning him.

He fumbled for his gun, pulled it from his shoulder holster, but she got in another hard blow with the duct-tape roll before he could even backhand her with the pistol.

He stumbled back, tripped over an icy rut and went down hard, knocking the air out of him. He managed to hang on to the weapon—he just couldn't get it aimed at her before she took off into the trees on one of the snow-mobile trails.

In the dim light, snow seemed to hang in the air, tiny crystals that danced around him as he struggled to his feet, torn between the pain from the fall and the raging anger caused by his injured pride and failure to kill Violet Evans.

She'd disappeared into the trees. He considered only a moment about going after her. He couldn't shoot her anyway. The report of the gunshot would echo across the mountain and alert Corbett.

~~Too bad~~ Claude wasn't here. He'd go after her. Claude, though, had been better at killing. He didn't mind the mess.

Ed swore under his breath as he slammed the trunk and headed back toward the open driver's side door. He was still furious. He liked things neatly tied up.

Maybe she would trip in the woods and break something and not be able to get back up, and freeze to death and they wouldn't find her body until spring.

That thought made him feel a little better as he slid behind the wheel of the car with a groan. He'd been shot and now hurt all over from the fall. Anger and frustration coursed through him, warming him. He stared out into the night, daring her to come back for more.

She didn't.

And after a few minutes, the cold crept back. He started the car and turned on the heater. The night wasn't as dark as nights in Texas because of the blanket of snow on everything.

And to make matters worse, it was snowing more

heavily now. At least it would make his approach more quiet, he thought as he drove back up the road a short way and pulled over.

He could see lights behind the dirty windows of the new cabin being built high up on the mountainside. He killed the engine and climbed out into the falling snow. The quiet was almost his undoing. He ached for Houston, the noise, the confusion of buildings and people.

He checked his weapon, then started up the mountain, following the tracks the pickup had left on the narrow road. It was time.

VIOLET HADN'T GONE FAR WHEN she'd fallen, tumbling down into a small, snow-filled gully. She lay there, staring up at the sky, angry and scared.

She didn't think he'd come after her. But then again she couldn't be sure of that. She pushed to her feet and heard the car drive off. He was leaving?

She listened, the sound of the car's big engine the only one on the mountainside.

He didn't go far before he pulled over. Then there was only the falling snow and silence.

Violet retraced her footsteps back to the empty snowmobile parking lot. Her head hurt, and she couldn't remember the last time she'd slept or eaten. It made her irritable.

"Forget about him. You have bigger fish to fry," her grandmother said beside her.

This time Violet didn't mind her grandmother being here. She didn't like being alone on this mountainside. It felt too quiet, too isolated and alone.

Also, she'd had a lot of time to think in the trunk without her grandmother's constant nagging. Her grandmother had never liked dark, cramped places so hadn't shown up until now.

"Someone put you in those places when you were a girl," Violet said with sudden insight. Her grandmother suddenly didn't seem as large next to her. "*Your* mother? Is that who did it to you? Why you did it to me when my mother wasn't around?"

"Are you going to stand around here and freeze to death or take care of business? Your mother—"

"Hated you, you evil old harpy." Violet could see her grandmother clearly now. The stooped shoulders, the drooping skin of her neck, the harsh, bitter line of her thin lips. But it was the eyes, dark and small as raisins, that had always glinted with malice.

Only now Violet saw something else behind the malice—misery and pain. The two fed off each other.

"Where are you going?"

Violet didn't answer. Nor did she look back. She walked up the road, leaving her dead grandmother standing in the ruts, snow falling all around her.

DEDE TURNED AND SAW LANTRY'S expression. Her heart began to pound. "What is it?" she asked as she stepped back over to him.

She'd been so disappointed in Frank that she hadn't wanted to touch the necklace. It disgusted her. She thought she'd known her husband. The stolen diamond necklace proved she never had.

"Lantry?"

He held the necklace up. The stones flashing in the firelight. "It's a fake."

"What?"

He handed the necklace to her. It felt heavy and cold.

"It's not even a good copy." His gaze came up to meet hers.

She felt as stunned as he looked as she studied the necklace in her hands and saw what he meant. "But I don't understand. Why would Frank hide worthless jewelry in the boat?"

Lantry was shaking his head as if equally perplexed by this turn of events. "Why get himself killed for this, unless he didn't realize he didn't have the real thing?"

"Frank wouldn't have been fooled. Not if this was the way he'd made his fortune to begin with. But why hide this in the boat and give it to you? It makes no sense."

"Or does it?" Lantry said.

Her eyes widened as they both seemed to come to the same conclusion. "Inside jobs?"

He nodded. "The homeowners had to be in on it. Which meant Frank was working with the people he robbed, stealing the phony jewelry, letting the homeowners collect the insurance and keep the real jewelry, paying Frank off with some of the insurance money."

Dede stared down at the necklace as a thought hit her. "But why would Frank keep this?"

"It's proof that the homeowner was in on the burglary," Lantry said. "These were wealthy people he was helping steal from the insurance companies. Is it possible he was blackmailing them later? He had the duplicate jewelry to prove they were in on the thefts."

Dede stared at the necklace, again feeling sick. "Quite an operation. But the last burglary was Tamara Fallon, his former assistant from the old days. Surely he wasn't planning to blackmail her." She felt Lantry staring at her and looked up to meet his eyes.

"Dede, didn't you say that Frank changed when Ed and Claude and Frank's former assistant, Tammy, turned up? Isn't it possible that Frank kept these particular duplicates to keep them from ever involving him again? I know it's a long shot, but if you were right and Frank really did want to change…"

She smiled at him, touched that he would try to put a good spin on this horrible situation.

"He had Tammy right where he wanted her as long as he had the duplicates stolen from her house," Lantry was saying. "It would prove she was in on the burglary, and if she really was in the middle of an ugly divorce and was trying to get as much money out—"

"But why would Ed and Claude go to so much trouble to try to get the duplicates back? Unless they think the necklace is the real thing. Isn't it possible that if Frank double-crossed Tammy, she double-crossed Ed and Claude?"

"Stranger things have happened. It might explain why Frank's dead and the police think they've found Tamara Fallon's body in a canal outside Houston."

Earlier, she'd heard a sound and thought it was the pop of the logs burning in the fireplace. But this time, she knew with certainty that the sound she heard hadn't just come from the fire—but from the back of the cabin.

As she turned, she saw a shadow fall across the floor. "Lantry—"

It was all she got out before the man stepped into the room and she saw the glint of the weapon in his hand.

He motioned to the necklace still entwined in her fingers. "I'll take that."

Chapter Twelve

All Lantry saw at first was the gun aimed at Dede's heart—and froze. The man holding the weapon was short and stocky, and Lantry had the feeling he'd seen him before.

"That's it, Mr. Corbett," the man said. "Don't do anything rash, or I'll have to shoot her."

"Let me guess. Ed, right?" Dede didn't sound afraid, and that amped up Lantry's fear for her twofold.

Ed gave a slight bow of his head in response. "I'll take that necklace now."

"You killed Frank for *this?*" Dede demanded, holding up the necklace. Lantry could hear the fury just under the surface. "You killed my husband for *this?*"

Ed shifted nervously as he watched Dede wind the necklace tighter around her fingers. "If you want to blame someone for Frank's death, you only have to look as far as that mirror on the wall."

Dede froze. "You're blaming me because *you* killed Frank?"

"Easy, Dede," Lantry warned, but he suspected she

wasn't listening. He could see the rage etched on her face. She closed her hand into a fist around the necklace.

"If he hadn't been so busy trying to protect you, he'd still be alive," Ed said, his own tone laced with anger. "I didn't want to kill Frank. But he forgot his loyalties. He betrayed us because of you."

Dede had her head cocked to one side, a stance Lantry had seen before. He didn't have to see the fire in her eyes to know that any moment she might launch herself at the man—to hell with the fact that he had a gun on her.

"He didn't betray you. He just didn't want any part of you or this burglary," she said, biting off each word.

"You don't know anything about Frank. He was one of us. He knew the cost of betrayal. He got greedy and wanted all the money for himself."

Dede opened her fist and let the necklace dangle from her fingers. "You think this was about money?"

"That necklace is worth almost two million dollars." His gaze flicked to Lantry. "Not chump change to some of us."

Just as they'd suspected, Ed didn't know the necklace was a worthless duplicate. Lantry thought it might be better to keep it that way.

Before Dede could spill the beans, Lantry jumped in. "There's no reason for bloodshed, Ed. You should have come to me right away. I'm a reasonable man. We could have made a deal for the necklace. It would have saved you a lot of time and effort. You wouldn't have had to kill Frank."

Ed seemed to relax a little, though he shifted his gaze to Dede every few seconds as if afraid of what she might do next. He wasn't the only one.

"We'd heard stories about you," Ed said. "We weren't sure you would be agreeable. But then, every man has his price, doesn't he?"

"Exactly. You could have cut me in. Much less messy that way."

Ed smiled. "A man who thinks like I do. I can appreciate that."

"Maybe it's not too late," Lantry said.

Ed laughed. "Under the circumstances, I'm not sure that's in my best interest."

Ed had killed Frank and probably Tamara Fallon. Clearly, the man had nothing to lose.

DEDE HAD BEEN SO FURIOUS SHE'D almost blown it. As her blood pressure dropped a little, she realized what Lantry had right away.

Ed thought the necklace was the real thing.

She blinked, feeling lightheaded. She couldn't help but think of Frank when she looked at this man. He'd killed her husband, and for what? A pile of worthless glass and metal.

She had wanted to scratch the man's eyes out and take her chances with the gun in his hand.

Irrational thinking. She was thankful that Lantry had kept his senses. Ed seemed amused by Lantry, although she could tell he was watching her out of the corner of his eye, not sure what she might do next.

Dede shivered and realized Ed had left the back door

open when he'd come in. That first sound she'd heard must have been him breaking the door lock.

She glanced toward the open doorway and the darkness beyond. Something moved through the falling snow behind him.

Someone else was out there.

"I'll take that necklace now. Nice and easy," Ed was saying.

"Why should we give it to you, knowing you plan to kill us either way?" Lantry asked.

"Like you said, there's no reason for more bloodshed," Ed said with a smile, lying through his teeth.

"What was it you had on Frank?" Dede asked.

Ed seemed surprised by the question. "Didn't he tell you?" He laughed. "No, of course, he didn't. He was ashamed." Ed's smile died abruptly. "Ashamed of his own brother."

"Brother?" Dede had barely gotten the word out when a figure materialized out of the snow and darkness behind Ed.

Dede felt a start as the person stepped into the dim light. Violet's face was bruised badly on one side of her face, her eye swollen and discolored. She carried something in her hands.

Dede didn't see what it was until she raised her arms and swung the large chunk of firewood at the back of Ed's head.

Ed must have sensed someone behind him or seen Dede's surprised expression. He started to turn, swinging around, leading with the gun.

Dede threw the necklace at him in a high arc. She saw

the indecision on his face. The fear that someone was behind him and the irresistible need to catch what he thought was an almost two-million-dollar diamond necklace.

Greed would have won out but he was half-turned, the gun already coming around to point at whatever was behind him. Ed twisted back, reaching with his free hand for the necklace as the chunk of firewood clutched in Violet's hands made contact with his skull.

Dede heard the thwack and the gunshot, both seeming simultaneous. Before she could move, Lantry grabbed her, taking her down to the floor, covering her with his body as a second shot was fired. She heard a cry, then the sound of a body hitting the floor.

It all happened in a heartbeat. Lantry was on his feet, Dede scrambling up after him.

The deafening sound of the gunshots echoed like cannon booms inside the cabin. Violet's cry of pain and the sound of Ed's body hitting the floor were followed by the thud of the chunk of firewood landing next to him.

Dede looked toward the doorway to find Ed lying at Violet's feet and Violet clutching her chest, her fingers blooming red with blood. Violet's gaze met her own as the older woman slowly dropped to her knees and fell forward beside Ed.

Lantry lunged for Ed, snatching the gun from his hand—but there was no need. Dede could see death in the dull glaze of his eyes. She shook off her inertia and rushed to Violet's side.

The woman had saved her life. Again.

"Violet? Violet, can you hear me?" Dede looked over at Lantry. "We have to get her to the hospital."

THE AMBULANCE AND SHERIFF'S deputies met them twenty miles out of Landusky. Dede sat in the back of the patrol car watching the falling snow as Violet was loaded onto a stretcher.

She could hear Lantry arguing with his brother outside the car.

"Damn it, Lantry, you don't know how lucky you are that you're not on *your* way to the jail," Shane said. "I fought like hell to get you released on your own recognizance pending further investigation into this case."

"You can't let them send Dede back to that mental hospital. She doesn't belong there. I'm telling you that all of this was her ex-husband's doing."

"She pulled a gun on a deputy and took you hostage at gunpoint."

"I'll say I went of my own free will."

Shane swore again. "Lantry, I'll see that she's protected, twenty-four seven, but I can tell you right now, she's got to go back to the hospital for a mental evaluation."

"I'll pay to have someone come here and do the evaluation," Lantry argued. "Help me with this, Shane. This woman is innocent. She's been through hell. If she hadn't come to Montana to warn me—"

"I'll see what I can do, all right?" Shane said, raising his voice over the sound of an ambulance taking off for Whitehorse.

Lantry climbed into the front of the patrol car and turned to look through the steel mesh at her.

"I hate to see you at odds with your brother," she said quietly.

He smiled and her heart took off at a gallop. "Shane and I are fine. It's you I'm worried about."

"Your brother's right. I'll be safe in jail. Both Ed and Claude are dead." Ed had confessed to killing Frank. Violet would back up her story about what happened in the van. There was that matter with the gun and the deputy, but even if she had to spend some time behind bars, she was just grateful that it was over and said as much to Lantry.

"It won't be over until you're cleared and free," he said with conviction. "You've been through enough."

His brother climbed behind the wheel and took off after the ambulance. Lantry fell silent. Dede watched the snowy landscape glide past as flakes fell like feathers from the ice-black sky overhead.

LANTRY SAT IN HIS BROTHER'S office, legs stretched out, his eyes dull from lack of sleep.

As Shane returned from down the hall with Dede, he stood up. Dede looked as awful as he felt. He drew her into his arms.

"Lantry, if you'll wait down the hall," Shane said to his brother after a moment. Lantry let go of Dede but didn't move.

"I'll be fine," she said.

He nodded and reluctantly left the room, closing the door behind him.

"I need to ask you some questions," Shane said. "I understand you hired a private investigator to follow your then-husband."

Dede nodded. "Jonathan O'Reilly."

"A private investigator by that name was found murdered the same week as your husband and Tamara Fallon. His office had been ransacked, all files and computers destroyed," Shane said.

Dede looked sick. "You don't think—"

"No, we don't believe you had anything to do with the murders, given the evidence we've uncovered."

"What kind of evidence?"

"You said Ed told you that Frank was his brother, right?" Shane asked.

"I'm sure he meant they'd been like brothers," Dede said.

"We ran the mental-hospital driver's fingerprints and were able to ID him from an old arrest record," Shane continued. "He was using an assumed name for employment at the hospital. His real name is Claude Ingram. Ed was his brother."

"Brothers?" Dede couldn't believe this.

"There's more," Shane said. "I checked into Frank Chamberlain's background, assuming he must have been from the same small Idaho town since you'd said they'd apparently known each other since childhood." Shane glanced at Dede. She nodded. "No Frank Chamberlain."

She felt herself pale.

"Both Claude and Ed were born in Idaho, a little town called Ashton. They had two other siblings. A sister and a brother."

Dede felt a chill even in the small, cramped room.

"Franklin John Ingram—"

Dede let out a gasp.

"—and Tamara Sue Ingram."

"Tammy was Frank's *sister?*" She stared at him for a moment, then shook her head. "That can't be possible. I thought Frank and Tamara…"

"Apparently they were in business together—both in security alarm systems and the burglaries of the clients' jewels," Shane said. "We're still waiting on DNA results, but from the identification found near the body, the woman found in the river was Tamara Fallon."

Dede shivered, remembering the photos of Tammy the PI had shown her. A slim, pretty woman with long blond hair pulled back in a ponytail and high cheekbones.

"No wonder Frank couldn't say no to them," Dede said. "Some family the Ingrams turned out to be. Is it any wonder Frank wanted to get away from them? Obviously he'd changed his name, thought he'd escaped them." She felt sick. "And now they are all dead."

AFTER SHANE HAD TAKEN THEIR statements separately, he got the call from the judge. He quickly realized just how small a town Whitehorse was and how things worked here.

Shane hung up and looked across the desk at Dede and Lantry. "Seems some strings have been pulled."

Dede would be remanded into Grayson Corbett's custody, fitted with a house-arrest device that would monitor her movements within a quarter-mile of the ranchhouse.

"How is Violet?" she asked Shane before she and Lantry left the sheriff's department.

"Looks like she's going to make it."

"Can I see her? She saved my life…and Lantry's."

Shane shook his head. "Only her mother has been allowed to see her. I can pass a message on to her mother for you."

"Just tell Violet thank you, all right? What she did was very brave." Or some might say crazy. Dede wondered why she'd done it. Why hadn't she just taken off and tried to save herself?

Kate Corbett put Dede up in the main house's guest suite and made her feel at home. Lantry was busy doing legal maneuvering, trying to keep them both out of jail, so she saw little of him that first day.

She couldn't believe it was almost Christmas Day. Trails West Ranch was decorated beautifully, and she knew that Kate had added several packages under the tree with Dede's name on them.

Dede wandered around the big house, feeling lost. She knew she was still in shock and dealing with everything that had happened. It saddened her how little she'd known about a man she'd married, and hated that Lantry might be right about marriage.

She'd loved Frank, planned to have his children. Now she was thankful she hadn't become pregnant.

Dede looked up to see a UPS truck pull up out front. A moment later Kate came into the room carrying a large package.

Kate had just gotten back from her knitting class in town and seemed more excited than usual. "I just found out that my daughters-in-law are all expecting! I'm going to have to learn to knit much faster if I hope to get baby buntings made before the grandbabies are all born."

Now Kate held out the package. "It's for you. It's from Lantry."

"Why would Lantry—"

"Open it," Kate said.

Dede tore open the box to find a beautiful guitar inside. Carefully she took it out. How had Lantry known? She felt tears rush to her eyes.

"You play?" Kate asked in confusion.

"I used to." Back before Frank, back before all of this. Her fingers ached to strum the strings, to make the music that used to fill her heart with such joy. "If you don't mind, I think I'll take it back to my room for now."

Kate nodded, looking concerned. "Is there anything I can do?"

Dede smiled and touched the woman's arm. Kate Corbett had been so kind to her. "Thank you, but I just need time to process everything that's happened. I feel that I got Lantry into this, and I—"

"Lantry and his profession got Lantry into this," Kate said, not unkindly. "Lantry took your husband's case. I would imagine he will always regret that." She smiled. "Except that it brought you into his life," she added quickly. "Otherwise, you two might never have met. I've seen the change in my stepson. Lantry had planned to go back to Texas right after Christmas, back to being a divorce lawyer. He won't do that now, you'll see. You've had a profound effect on him."

Dede smiled at that. "I almost got him killed. Have you heard anything on Violet Evans?"

"She's being moved to a private mental hospital close by right after the wedding Christmas Day," Kate said.

"Arlene is marrying Hank Monroe tomorrow. Arlene got special permission for her daughter to attend the wedding."

As she carried the guitar Lantry had given her down to her room, Dede thought about what Kate had said. They'd all been changed by what had happened. Would Lantry really give up his career because of it?

Once in her room, Dede ran her fingers lovingly across the guitar strings. She hadn't played in so long. Slowly, she picked up the guitar, her fingers remembering the music as she began to play.

LANTRY HAD A LOT ON HIS MIND. In a word: Dede. At first he'd been so busy trying to get her cleared that he hadn't had time to think about the future. Her mental evaluation had gone well. Now, if he could just work his legal magic, Dede would be free to return to Texas after Christmas.

The duplicate necklace and both his and Dede's statements, along with evidence that continued to come in on the Ingram siblings, had forced a judge in Texas to take another look at Dede's commitment to the mental hospital.

Just after the holidays, a local judge would rule on the other charges against Dede.

There would be nothing keeping Dede in Montana after that. Nothing keeping him, either, for that matter.

He had come so close to being disbarred. It surprised him that he wasn't more upset about that. But he realized he had no interest in returning to his law practice in Texas. Or returning to Texas at all.

He could sell his practice, walk away with a nice chunk of change, and then what?

He knew he was at a crossroads, but not one where he'd

ever been before. For the first time in his life, he didn't know what he was going to do tomorrow or the next day.

He thought about his father's offer. "There's some good grazing land that will be coming up for sale soon to the south. If you were interested in staying, I sure could use your help."

"Dad, I...I'm not sure what I'm going to do," he'd said truthfully.

"This case has changed your mind about being a divorce lawyer?"

Lantry had chuckled. "You could say that."

"Or is it the woman?"

"A lot of both," he'd found himself admitting.

"Are you in love with her?"

Lantry had looked at his father, realizing this talk was Kate's doing, since it was so unlike his father to ask such a question. "Dede's still in love with her ex-husband."

"Oh." His father had looked uncomfortable. "Kate seems to think Dede's in love with you. Kate's seldom wrong about these things."

Lantry had laughed. "And she told you to talk to me."

His father had laughed as well. "She might have suggested I mention that land I was thinking about buying. Said there was a beautiful spot down that way for a house." Grayson had shrugged, unapologetic for trying. "You're a cowboy, son. It's in your blood."

That it was, Lantry thought as he drove toward the ranch, anxious to see Dede.

THE HOUSE WAS QUIET, Juanita in the kitchen, Kate in her study, knitting. Dede felt restless and more anxious by the hour. Not about going to jail, for she knew Lantry would move heaven and earth so that didn't happen.

No, it was about leaving Montana—and Lantry.

They hadn't been together since the cabin in Landusky. She had seen Lantry struggling when he was around her.

"He's in love with you," Kate told her that morning when she caught Dede watching Lantry leave the house.

Dede had laughed and shook her head. "I'm sorry, but you're wrong."

Kate had smiled a knowing smile. "He doesn't know how to handle it, since he's never felt like this before. Trust me. He's in love with you. Look how hard he's working to get you cleared of all the charges. Right now he's trying to get that stupid house-arrest device off your ankle before Christmas day."

Now Dede stood at the window, remembering Kate's words. Lantry had definitely spent every waking hour since her arrest trying to get her freed. But she suspected he liked the work because it kept him from having to deal with his feelings, deal with her.

"Lantry thinks you're still in love with your ex-husband," Kate had said.

"The man I fell in love with didn't really exist," Dede had told her. "It's hard to explain how I feel about Frank. Empty. Sad. Disappointed. Sorry. I suppose a part of me still loves the man Frank could have been, the man he wanted to be."

Kate had smiled and hugged her. "You and I have more in common than you might think. I loved a man when I was young. He let me down. It is only now that

I realize he never was the man I wanted or needed him to be. But I mourned for years for what that love could have been. As women it isn't easy to let go of those dreams, is it?"

"No, it isn't," Dede said to herself now. Just as it wasn't going to be easy to leave this place, to leave Kate and the rest of the family who had welcomed her so lovingly. Or to leave Lantry.

Just as it wouldn't be easy to spend Christmas here with all of them, knowing she would be leaving as soon as the holidays were over.

Since her father's death, Dede had pretty much ignored Christmas other than to go to church on Christmas Eve.

Kate had insisted Dede stay through the holidays even if Lantry was able to get her exonerated. Kate had been right about one thing: there was nothing waiting for Dede in Texas.

She pressed her fingers against the cool glass of the window as she looked out over the ranch. A Chinook had blown in, the warm wind melting off the snow. The weatherman had promised a white Christmas, though, warning of another storm coming in tonight.

Lantry hadn't managed to get her freed of the house-arrest device on her ankle, but he had asked that she be given a larger area to roam.

She watched one of the mares running around the corral as if enjoying the feel of the warm wind. Dede thought about telling Kate she was going to walk down to the corral, but didn't want to disturb her when she was concentrating so hard on her knitting.

The wind was warm and smelled of spring—an

illusion, since winter had only begun. Growing up in Wyoming, Dede remembered days like this that teased and tempted.

The sun was low, the daylight fading fast. She wondered when Lantry would be home. Late, she was sure. As she walked, Dede listened to the wind in the large pines. The Christmas lights swung to and fro on the branches.

The mare came right over to her. Dede reached in her pocket and took out the apple she'd gotten from Juanita and offered it to the horse.

"You're sure pretty," she said to the horse as the mare chomped the apple then snuffled her hand and pocket to see if there were any more.

Dede felt a sliver of trepidation at the thought of someday enjoying riding again, but Kate had told her this mare was gentle, and as she rubbed its neck she thought the mare wanted to go as badly as she did.

"How about I see if I can round up some tack?" she told the mare. "The best I can do is a ride around the corral, but if you're up for it, so am I." The mare whinnied.

Dede headed for the barn, the mare trailing along beside her inside the corral.

It was dark in the big old barn. Dede felt around for a light, snapped it on. Inside the cavernous barn, she could still hear the howl of the wind. It was cooler in here, cold compared to the warm wind and waning sunlight outside.

She walked through the barn toward the stalls and found the tack room. She didn't hurry and knew part of it was fear.

It had been different riding the two horses she'd borrowed to escape. Greater fears had driven her.

She didn't have to ride ever again. She heard the mare whinny at the corral fence at the other end of the barn.

Dede laughed as she dragged out a halter and horse blanket and was checking out the array of saddles when she heard the barn door open and close. The wind? Or had Lantry returned and come looking for her?

Her heart did a little flip.

She listened. *Must just have been the wind,* she thought, disappointed. Dede reached for one of the saddles.

The barn lights went out.

Chapter Thirteen

Lantry was almost to the ranch when his cell phone vibrated in his jacket pocket. He realized as he reached for the phone that he was hoping it was Dede. He knew he'd been avoiding her. Giving her space, is what he'd told himself.

Sending her the guitar had been one of those spur-of-the-moment decisions. Now that he'd done it, though, he was excited to hear her play.

Just the thought of talking to her made his heart beat a little faster and—

It wasn't Dede, but Shane.

"Hey," he said into the phone, reining in his disappointment as he stopped at the top of a hill to take the call, fearing it was about Dede's case and knowing he was going to want all his concentration on that—not driving.

"I have some news I thought you'd want to hear right away," Shane said, tension in his voice that set Lantry on edge.

"That body found in the canal in Texas wasn't Tamara Fallon's."

Lantry let that sink in. "I thought the police found ID—"

"Given what we know now, the Houston police think she might have tried to fake her death so she could get away with the diamond necklace."

There was more. Lantry could feel it.

"A woman matching Tamara Fallon's description flew into Billings last night," Shane said. "Lantry, the Houston police told me that her husband, Dr. Eric Fallon, said his wife was obsessed with one of her brother's wives, and since Frank was the only one who was married…"

That disquiet was now full-blown worry. "You're saying Tamara Fallon flew to Montana because of Dede?"

"Dr. Fallon seems to think that Tamara blames Dede for Frank turning his back on her and his brothers."

Lantry glanced toward the Little Rockies in the distance. "I'm almost back to the ranch. I've got to go." He snapped off the phone and hit the gas. Everyone had planned to be away from the ranch house today except for Dede, Kate and Juanita.

As he topped the next rise in the road, he saw the smoke.

"HEY!" DEDE CALLED OUT. "MIND turning the lights back on?" No lights. No answer. "Hello?" She hated that her voice broke. The barn had taken on a weighty silence, and she realized she wasn't alone anymore.

But why didn't whoever had turned out the lights say something? The Corbett brothers joked and kidded around with each other, but they weren't big practical jokers, and this wasn't funny.

She looked around for something to use as a weapon, telling herself she was just being silly. She couldn't trust her emotions after everything she'd been through. Especially after falling for Lantry Corbett.

That thought stopped her cold for a moment. She'd fallen in love with him. Why had it taken until this moment to admit that?

"Hello?" she called again, praying someone would answer as she spotted a pitchfork stuck in a hay bale in one of the stalls.

She took a step in the growing darkness of the barn toward the pitchfork, then another, trying not to make a sound as she listened. She could hear nothing over the howl of the wind outside.

The barn had filled with deep shadows. She caught the scent of perfume just an instant before the figure stepped out of an adjacent stall in front of her—blocking her way out.

A flashlight beam snapped on, blinding her. She flinched, heard a chuckle, then the beam dropped to the barn floor.

Tamara Fallon had changed her hair color. She was no longer a blond. Her hair was short and dark. But the face was the same one Dede had seen in the photographs the private investigator had shown her.

"Frank told me you were pretty," Tamara said. "In a sweet way." She made *sweet* sound like a dirty word.

Dede could see the resemblance, though slight between the siblings. She was too startled to speak, and while Tamara wasn't brandishing anything more deadly than a flashlight, she sensed that the woman was dangerous.

"What's wrong? Thought I was dead?" The woman's laugh was sharp as a blade.

"I'm just surprised to see you here," Dede said truthfully. Surprised and fearful.

"Did you know that Frank and I were fraternal twins?" Tamara shook her head. "I didn't think so. Your private investigator died before he could tell you that, huh? There's no stronger bond than the bond between twins."

"I've heard that," Dede said, reasoning that antagonizing this woman would be a mistake. No one knew Dede had gone down to the barn, and she wasn't sure when it would be discovered that she was missing, since she was able to go at least as far as the barn.

She wondered if Tamara knew about the house-arrest tracking device strapped to her ankle. Dede's jeans covered it. The alarm would go off at the sheriff's department if she went only a few yards farther than the back of the barn.

Tamara hadn't threatened her. Not yet, anyway. But Dede had already decided that she would have to find a way to step out of her specified area—and soon. Something about the woman's demeanor warned her that Tamara's visit wasn't a friendly one.

"So you probably wonder what I'm doing in Montana," Tamara said, glancing around the barn. "Aren't you the least bit curious?"

Dede could tell that the woman was watching her out of the corner of her eye. "Not really. I should get back to the house. Everyone will be looking for me."

Tamara laughed. "Not likely, since there was a fire

behind the house and both women are out there right now fighting it in that awful wind. Wouldn't it be a shame if the blaze burned all the way down here to the barn?"

Dede's heart fell at the thought of Kate and Juanita being in danger because of her. As she caught the smell of smoke, she glanced toward the end of the barn. The mare was still standing there, waiting. Behind the horse, the horizon was an odd color, almost pink in the darkening sky. The snowstorm. It was probably already snowing in the Little Rockies.

If she could make a break for it, run to the end of the barn and out into the corral—

Dede felt the full weight of the woman's gaze. "My brothers are dead because of you."

The mare had picked up the scent of the smoke and was moving nervously. Dede shifted on her feet, saw Tamara tense.

Dede knew she had to do something. Now. "You blame *me* for your brothers' deaths?" she demanded, taking a step toward the woman.

Tamara reacted instinctively by taking a step back. The move gave Dede a little more room for when the time came to run.

"Your *brothers* tried to kill me," Dede said.

Tamara was clearly taken aback by this confrontational manner of Dede's. She had obviously expected Dede to cower in fear. Not that Dede wasn't shaking in her boots. She just couldn't let Tamara see that fear.

But there was also an underlying anger. Because of this woman who professed such a bond with her brother, Frank was dead. She said as much to the woman.

"He'd be alive if he hadn't married you and betrayed his own family," Tamara shot back. "You turned him against us. You poisoned his mind. Frank would never have—"

"Double-crossed you otherwise?" Dede demanded. "The police have the duplicate necklace. They know about the other burglaries. They'll soon figure out who masterminded all of it—including killing Frank and sending your other brothers after a worthless necklace and to their deaths."

Tamara looked livid. Spittle came out of her mouth when she finally was able to speak. "You bitch."

Dede knew the woman would go for her throat. She'd been ready. As Tamara charged, she stepped to the side, managing to trip her up. Tamara stumbled. Dede didn't look back as she ran toward the end of the barn.

She just hoped this monitoring device worked.

But even if it alerted the sheriff's department, it would take someone awhile to get out to the ranch, and Dede was all out of a plan to escape as she heard Tamara shout for her to stop.

Dede had almost reached the end of the barn when the wood of one of the stall supports splintered in front of her as a popping sound echoed through the large old barn. Another pop.

Dede felt a sharp pain in her side, felt her feet stumble. Something was wrong. Her hand went to her side and came away covered in blood.

THE PICKUP ROARED INTO THE ranch yard. Lantry was out of it before the truck came to a stop. He ran toward where his stepmother and Juanita were dousing the last of the flames.

The dried grasses of fall had made perfect tinder for the flames that skittered across the back of the house chased by the wind.

But the two women had managed to narrow the blaze and now had it almost out.

"Lantry," Kate cried over the wind when she saw him. She had one of the fire extinguishers kept at the back door. Juanita was manning the garden hose. "We can't find Dede. I think she's down at the barn."

He could hear a horse whinnying. It had smelled the smoke.

"Go find her," Kate ordered.

He took off at a run as an unsettling thought lodged itself in his gut. Dede had grown up on a ranch. The moment she smelled the smoke, she would have come running. Wildfires were always a fear.

As he neared the barn, he saw the horse in the corral. It ran in a tight nervous circle. There was no way Dede wouldn't have heard the horse if she was in the barn.

He burst into the barn, surprised to find it dark inside. Reaching for the switch, he snapped on the lights and blinked.

"Dede!"

"Down here" came a female voice he didn't recognize.

"Lantry, no, she has a gun!"

The chilling sound of Dede's words rattled through him. He took a step, then another in the direction her voice had come from.

"Tamara?" he said as he neared the back end of the barn. "I heard you were in town."

"Good news travels fast," she shot back with a laugh that turned his blood to ice.

"Are you all right, Dede?" he asked, trying to keep the panic out of his voice.

"She's bleeding like a stuck pig," Tamara answered. "But she's still alive. Why don't you join us?"

That was exactly what he planned to do. He wasn't about to let Dede spend another second alone with the woman.

As he drew closer, he saw a pair of jean-clad legs protruding from the end stall.

"That's close enough," Tamara said and peered around the end of the stall nearer Dede's feet.

It wasn't near close enough, so he kept walking.

"Are you hard of hearing?" Tamara asked. "I said that was close enough."

He kept coming. So far he hadn't seen the weapon Tamara had used to shoot Dede. The stall walls were tall enough that she'd have a hell of a hard time shooting him over one of them. She'd have to step out and take aim. That meant he would have a few seconds before she fired.

"I said stop!" Tamara's voice rose, shrill even in the echo.

He was almost to her, coming fast. He knew he couldn't give her time to think. She had to fear him. If she had time to think, she would threaten Dede—the only thing that could hold him back. Instead, he had to make her fear for her own life if he reached her. He had to get her to turn the gun on him.

Tamara stepped out of the stall, leading with the barrel of the pistol just as he'd hoped she would. He was so close now that she didn't have enough time to aim. The gun made a popping sound. Wood splintered on the stall door next to him.

She tried to fire again, but she'd forgotten momentarily about Dede. Dede kicked Tamara's feet out from under her. A grunt escaped the woman's lips as she hit the ground, going down hard.

The gun popped again. Dust sifted down from the barn ceiling. But by then, Lantry was on her, twisting the weapon from her fingers and pointing the barrel at Tamara as he dropped beside Dede.

"Are you all right?" he cried, seeing her lying in the straw bed of the stall holding her side, her angelic face pinched with pain.

She nodded and smiled. "I am now."

He started to pull out his cell phone to call his brother, but before he could, he heard sirens. He looked up confusion at Dede.

She pointed to her ankle monitor. The light was flashing. She'd managed to set it off.

"Nice work," Lantry said. As the barn filled with uniformed officers, he handed over Tamara Ingram Fallon's weapon and lifted Dede into his arms. "I'm not waiting for an ambulance," he said to his brother. "I'm taking her myself."

Chapter Fourteen

Dede woke Christmas morning to find Lantry sleeping in a chair next to her bed.

"Good morning, sleepyhead," he said, opening his eyes.

She couldn't believe this cowboy. After the doctor told him that her gunshot wound wasn't serious, he'd hired a nurse and brought her back to the ranch.

"It's Christmas. I'm not having you spend it in a hospital," he'd told her.

"How are you feeling?" he asked now.

After waking up to find him next to her bed? Wonderful. "A little sore, but other than that, pretty good."

He smiled. He really did have a great smile. "Ready for Christmas?" He sounded like a kid, anxious to see what Santa Claus had left him under the tree.

"Ready," Dede whispered as Lantry carried her into the living room. All the family was gathered around the tree.

Dede smelled hot apple cider. It mingled with the scent of evergreen. Outside it was one of those amazing Montana days. All blue sky and sunshine, making last night's fresh snowfall glitter like diamonds.

For just a moment she couldn't help but think of Frank. She felt nothing of the old pain, only a twinge of sadness. Her heart didn't ache. It felt like a helium balloon allowed to fly free again, she thought as she looked over at Lantry.

All around her there was laughter mingling with the sound of happy chatter. *These Corbetts,* Dede thought, shaking her head. *What a big, boisterous family.* The kind she'd always dreamed of being a part of.

She wiped at a tear, caught Lantry looking over at her with concern.

"Are you sure you're up to this?" he whispered, leaning close.

"I wouldn't miss this for the world." She smiled at him and hastily brushed away the moisture at the corner of her eye.

For a moment she thought he was going to kiss her.

The room seemed to have gone quiet, everything stopping in midmotion. All she could hear was her heart in her chest banging like a drum as she looked into Lantry's blue eyes and remembered the tickle of his mustache, the feel of his lips on hers.

"Better open this one," someone said, handing her a present. The room came alive again as Lantry leaned back, the moment lost.

Dede watched as the family tore into the presents spilling out from around the tree. There were ohhs and ahhs and laughter and hugs as the pile of paper and ribbons grew.

Kate had been kind enough to do some shopping for Dede since she couldn't leave the ranch with her monitoring device. The older woman smiled over at her now as family members opened the presents she'd bought from Dede. Kate had great taste, and Dede smiled back her thanks.

"Well, is that it?" Grayson asked as the frenzy slowed down. The family was sprawled around the tree, many sporting their presents of new slippers or sweaters. "Then let's have breakfast."

Everyone started getting up to head into the large dining room. The talk turned to Juanita's Christmas Day breakfast. It sounded like quite a spread.

Lantry didn't move until everyone else had left but he and Dede. "That's not quite it," he said as he got to his feet and went to the tree. From deep in the thick green boughs he took out a small velvet box.

Dede felt her heart set off at a gallop as Lantry came back over to the chair where she sat and knelt down in front of her. She was already shaking her head.

"Dede, there are some things I have to say. I used to figure if two people were stupid enough to get married, then they deserved whatever happened to them."

"Like me and Frank."

He shook his head. "Frank loved you. I believe that. He wouldn't have changed his name and tried to make a new life with you if he hadn't. You made him want to be a better person. It wasn't your fault that his family had such a hold over him."

"That whole 'blood is thicker than water' thing?"

He nodded. "I can't go back to what I used to do. I'm not cynical enough about love and marriage anymore. It's not a requirement for being a divorce lawyer, but it helps."

She let out a nervous laugh. For a while she'd been so afraid to dream that Lantry might feel the same way about her that she felt about him.

He pulled her close. "I'd never known what falling in love felt like. I had no idea the crazy thoughts that come into your head. It's no wonder people get married. Wait, I'm not saying this right."

He took her hand. Behind him, the lights of the Christmas tree glittered brightly. Somewhere in the house, "Silent Night" was playing. The room seemed magical, something out of a fairy tale.

"Lantry, what are you doing?" she asked, scared.

"I'm trying to ask you to marry me," he said, his voice breaking. "This is just our first Christmas together. But I want to spend the rest of them with you. I love you, Dede. I want to marry you."

She couldn't believe this. *"Marriage?"* Had he really said the M word?

"I'm as surprised as you are. I never thought this day would come. But then, I'd never met anyone like you. I can't imagine a life without you in it."

"Aren't you worried about the odds of us making it?" she had to ask, fearing this couldn't be real.

He shook his head. "You and I are going to be in that fifty percent who spend our lives together and die within days of each other when we are old because we can't stand to live without the other."

She couldn't help but smile. "That sounds awfully romantic, cowboy."

He grinned and placed the small velvet box in the palm of her hand. "I know it's too soon. I know you're going to need time. But I can't let you just walk out of my life."

"This is happening too fast," she said, unable to trust this moment. Hadn't her heart wanted this? Ached for this from the moment she'd fallen in love with this man?

"I know. That's why I'm suggesting a long engagement. Not for me," he added quickly, with a laugh. "If you'd have me, I'd marry you this afternoon right here in front of this Christmas tree."

She touched his handsome face. "This is so not like you."

"I know, but, Dede, I want to be that couple who wears out their wedding bands from years of marriage. I want that with you. I believe you and I can have that kind of marriage, or I wouldn't ask you. Just say you'll think about it and that you won't go back to Texas."

She raised an eyebrow. "Are you saying you're staying on here at the ranch?"

"My father is expanding the ranch. He's offered me a job and some land south of here for a house."

Dede wanted to pinch herself. Being here on the Trails West Ranch had reminded her how much she'd missed the ranch she'd grown up on. How much she'd missed this country and the lifestyle. She might even get over her fear of horses—with Lantry's help.

With his love, she knew there was nothing she couldn't do.

"DON'T MAKE UP YOUR MIND right now," Lantry said, his heart in his throat. He knew it was too early. He also knew she'd been hurt too badly by her first marriage. She would be afraid to trust.

But he couldn't just let her walk out of his life.

She looked down at the box in her palm.

"You can open it if you'd like. Or you can wait until you're ready." He wanted her to open it. Hell, he wanted her to accept his proposal and wear the ring.

Slowly, she opened the box and let out a small gasp.

"The ring belonged to my grandmother. She and my grandfather were married sixty-three years. I figured if it worked for them..." He shrugged.

Dede leaned down and kissed him. "It is *perfect*."

"Does that mean you'll marry me?"

"One day, I will, yes."

Epilogue

The weddings of the last of the two Corbett brothers were huge affairs, with everyone in three counties invited.

There was dancing and Mexican food and a celebration that lasted for several days. Weeks later, everyone was still talking about how pretty the brides had been and how handsome those Corbett brothers were.

Lantry looked up to see his father framed in the doorway. "Dad?"

Grayson seemed to hesitate before he stepped into the room. "I suppose you'll be going back to Texas now that the wedding is over and you're back from your honeymoon."

So that explained his father's serious look.

"Actually," Lantry said, smiling at his father, "I've decided not to go back to being a divorce lawyer. I figure I'd better stay around my family given how much trouble this family gets into."

His father registered surprise. "I just assumed since Dede is from Texas…"

"Well, you know she grew up on a ranch in Wyoming.

So this country up here feels more like home to her than Texas ever did."

His father grinned. "I couldn't be more pleased. I think I mentioned that there's a nice section to the south that would be a perfect place for a house. But in the meantime, no reason for you two not to stay in one of the cabins close by."

Lantry laughed. His father had gotten what he wanted, what their mother had wanted. The Corbett family had all settled in Montana on the Trails West Ranch. Not only would Grayson have his family close by, he now had five daughters-in-law—all strong-willed and independent—and grandbabies on the way.

"So tell me, Dad. Was there ever really any letters from our mother?"

Grayson smiled. "You were always such a skeptic. I suppose you were destined to be a lawyer—at least for a while." He reached into his inside jacket pocket and pulled out a yellowed envelope. "This one is for you, son."

Lantry saw his name printed on the front in a small, neat hand. His heart dipped and rose as he took the letter from the mother he could barely remember.

"I just gave your brothers theirs," Grayson said. "They wanted to wait until you all were married and had your letters before they opened them. I'll leave you to it," he said and left him alone.

Lantry turned the envelope over in his fingers. He had one clear memory of his mother he'd held on to all these years. It was of her leaning into his crib and touching his cheek as she sang softly.

He carefully opened the envelope and slipped out the single sheet of paper.

To my dearest Lantry,

And suddenly he could hear her sweet voice, feel the brush of her fingers across his cheek, the memory coming alive again as his heart swelled and his eyes filled with tears.

For a few minutes he had his mother back.

He just wished she'd lived long enough to see this day. Her wish had come true. All five of her sons were happily married to cowgirls—or at least women who were fast becoming Montana cowgirls.

Carefully, he put the letter back in the envelope and went to find his wife. His wife. He smiled at the memory of Dede in her wedding dress standing next to him before the altar. Some day she would sing to their babies.

He headed out the door of the main ranchhouse. He knew he'd find her down at the corrals with the new mare. What she didn't know was that the horse was her wedding present, and one day she would ride again.

When he saw her leaning on the corral fence, his heart filled with so much joy and love he thought he might explode. A man didn't deserve to be this happy.

As he watched her, the sun in her hair, lighting her blue eyes, he remembered something his father had once told him. A horse always knows its way home. So does a cowboy.

*Celebrate 60 years of pure reading pleasure
with Harlequin®!*

To commemorate the event, Silhouette Special
Edition invites you to Ashley O'Ballivan's bed-
and-breakfast in the small town of Stone Creek.
The beautiful innkeeper will have her hands full
caring for her old flame Jack McCall. He's on the
run and recovering from a mysterious illness, but
that won't stop him from trying to win Ashley back.

*Enjoy an exclusive glimpse of Linda Lael Miller's
AT HOME IN STONE CREEK
Available in November 2009
from Silhouette Special Edition®*

Ashley, would take him in whatever her misgivings.

He had to get to Ashley; he'd be all right.

The helicopter swung abruptly sideways in a dizzying arch, setting Jack McCall's fever-ravaged brain spinning.

His friend's voice sounded tinny, coming through the earphones. "You belong in a hospital," he said. "Not some backwater bed-and-breakfast."

All Jack really knew about the virus raging through his system was that it wasn't contagious, and there was no known treatment for it besides a lot of rest and quiet. "I don't like hospitals," he responded, hoping he sounded like his normal self. "They're full of sick people."

Vince Griffin chuckled but it was a dry sound, rough at the edges. "What's in Stone Creek, Arizona?" he asked. "Besides a whole lot of nothin'?"

Ashley O'Ballivan was in Stone Creek, and she was a whole lot of somethin', but Jack had neither the strength nor the inclination to explain. After the way he'd ducked out six months before, he didn't expect a welcome, knew he didn't deserve one. But Ashley, being Ashley, would take him in whatever her misgivings.

He had to get to Ashley; he'd be all right.

He closed his eyes, letting the fever swallow him.

There was no telling how much time had passed when he became aware of the chopper blades slowing overhead. Dimly, he saw the private ambulance waiting on the airfield outside of Stone Creek; it seemed that twilight had descended.

Jack sighed with relief. His clothes felt clammy against his flesh. His teeth began to chatter as two figures unloaded a gurney from the back of the ambulance and waited for the blades to stop.

"Great," Vince remarked, unsnapping his seat belt. "Those two look like volunteers, not real EMTs."

The chopper bounced sickeningly on its runners, and Vince, with a shake of his head, pushed open his door and jumped to the ground, head down.

Jack waited, wondering if he'd be able to stand on his own. After fumbling unsuccessfully with the buckle on his seat belt, he decided not.

When it was safe the EMTs approached, following Vince, who opened Jack's door.

His old friend Tanner Quinn stepped around Vince, his grin not quite reaching his eyes.

"You look like hell warmed over," he told Jack cheerfully.

"Since when are you an EMT?" Jack retorted.

Tanner reached in, wedged a shoulder under Jack's right arm and hauled him out of the chopper. His knees immediately buckled, and Vince stepped up, supporting him on the other side.

"In a place like Stone Creek," Tanner replied, "everybody helps out."

They reached the wheeled gurney, and Jack found himself on his back.

Tanner and the second man strapped him down, a process that brought back a few bad memories.

"Is there even a hospital in this place?" Vince asked irritably from somewhere in the night.

"There's a pretty good clinic over in Indian Rock," Tanner answered easily, "and it isn't far to Flagstaff." He paused to help his buddy hoist Jack and the gurney into the back of the ambulance. "You're in good hands, Jack. My wife is the best veterinarian in the state."

Jack laughed raggedly at that.

Vince muttered a curse.

Tanner climbed into the back beside him, perched on some kind of fold-down seat. The other man shut the doors.

"You in any pain?" Tanner said as his partner climbed into the driver's seat and started the engine.

"No." Jack looked up at his oldest and closest friend and wished he'd listened to Vince. Ever since he'd come down with the virus—a week after snatching a five-year-old girl back from her non-custodial parent, a small-time Colombian drug dealer—he hadn't been able to think about anyone or anything but Ashley. When he *could* think, anyway.

Now, in one of the first clearheaded moments he'd experienced since checking himself out of Bethesda the day before, he realized he might be making a major mistake. Not by facing Ashley—he owed her that much and a lot more. No, he could be putting her in danger, putting Tanner and his daughter and his pregnant wife in danger, too.

"I shouldn't have come here," he said, keeping his voice low.

Tanner shook his head, his jaw clamped down hard as though he was irritated by Jack's statement.

"This is where you belong," Tanner insisted. "If you'd had sense enough to know that six months ago, old buddy, when you bailed on Ashley without so much as a fare-thee-well, you wouldn't be in this mess."

Ashley. The name had run through his mind a million times in those six months, but hearing somebody say it out loud was like having a fist close around his insides and squeeze hard.

Jack couldn't speak.

Tanner didn't press for further conversation.

The ambulance bumped over country roads, finally hitting smooth blacktop.

"Here we are," Tanner said. "Ashley's place."

* * * * *

Will Jack be able to
patch things up with Ashley,
or will his past put the woman he loves
in harm's way?
Find out in
AT HOME IN STONE CREEK
by Linda Lael Miller
Available November 2009
from Silhouette Special Edition®

This November,
Silhouette Special Edition®
brings you

NEW YORK TIMES
BESTSELLING AUTHOR

LINDA LAEL
MILLER

At Home in
Stone Creek

*Available in November
wherever books are sold.*

FROM *NEW YORK TIMES*
BESTSELLING AUTHOR

DIANA
PALMER

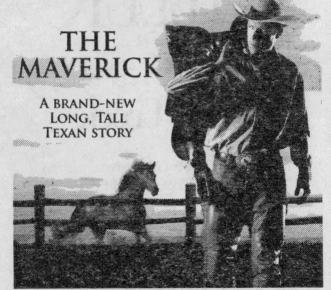

THE
MAVERICK

A BRAND-NEW
LONG, TALL
TEXAN STORY

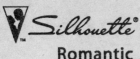

Silhouette®

Romantic
SUSPENSE

**Sparked by Danger,
Fueled by Passion.**

---

*Blackout
At Christmas*

Beth Cornelison,
Sharron McClellan,
Jennifer Morey

What happens when a major blackout shuts
down the entire Western seaboard on Christmas
Eve? Follow stories of danger, intrigue and
romance as three women learn to trust their
instincts to survive and open their hearts to the
love that unexpectedly comes their way.

**Available November
wherever books are sold.**

Visit Silhouette Books at www.eHarlequin.com

SRS27653

nocturne™

TIME RAIDERS
THE PROTECTOR

by *USA TODAY* bestselling author
MERLINE LOVELACE

Former USAF officer Cassandra Jones's unique psychic skills come in handy, as she has been selected to join the elite Time Raiders squad. Her first mission is to travel back to seventh-century China to locate the final piece of a missing bronze medallion. Major Max Brody is assigned to accompany her, and soon Cassandra and Max have to fight their growing attraction to each other while the mission suddenly turns deadly....

Available November
wherever books are sold.

REQUEST YOUR FREE BOOKS!

2 FREE NOVELS
PLUS 2
FREE GIFTS!

🛡 HARLEQUIN®

INTRIGUE®

Breathtaking Romantic Suspense

YES! Please send me 2 FREE Harlequin Intrigue® novels and my 2 FREE gifts (gifts are worth about $10). After receiving them, if I don't wish to receive any more books, I can return the shipping statement marked "cancel." If I don't cancel, I will receive 6 brand-new novels every month and be billed just $4.24 per book in the U.S. or $4.99 per book in Canada. That's a savings of close to 15% off the cover price! It's quite a bargain! Shipping and handling is just 50¢ per book.* I understand that accepting the 2 free books and gifts places me under no obligation to buy anything. I can always return a shipment and cancel at any time. Even if I never buy another book from Harlequin, the two free books and gifts are mine to keep forever.

182 HDN EYTR 382 HDN EYT3

Name	(PLEASE PRINT)	
Address		Apt. #
City	State/Prov.	Zip/Postal Code

Signature (if under 18, a parent or guardian must sign)

Mail to the **Harlequin Reader Service:**
IN U.S.A.: P.O. Box 1867, Buffalo, NY 14240-1867
IN CANADA: P.O. Box 609, Fort Erie, Ontario L2A 5X3

Not valid to current subscribers of Harlequin Intrigue books.

**Are you a current subscriber of Harlequin Intrigue books
and want to receive the larger-print edition?
Call 1-800-873-8635 today!**

* Terms and prices subject to change without notice. Prices do not include applicable taxes. Sales tax applicable in N.Y. Canadian residents will be charged applicable provincial taxes and GST. Offer not valid in Quebec. This offer is limited to one order per household. All orders subject to approval. Credit or debit balances in a customer's account(s) may be offset by any other outstanding balance owed by or to the customer. Please allow 4 to 6 weeks for delivery. Offer available while quantities last.

Your Privacy: Harlequin is committed to protecting your privacy. Our Privacy Policy is available online at www.eHarlequin.com or upon request from the Reader Service. From time to time we make our lists of customers available to reputable third parties who may have a product or service of interest to you. If you would prefer we not share your name and address, please check here. ☐

HI09R

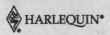

INTRIGUE

COMING NEXT MONTH

Available November 10, 2009

#1167 BRAVO, TANGO, COWBOY by Joanna Wayne
Special Ops Texas
The svelte dancer caught the cowboy's eye on the dance floor, but as the former navy SEAL joins in the search for her kidnapped daughter, she may just steal his heart, as well.

#1168 THE COLONEL'S WIDOW? by Mallory Kane
Black Hills Brotherhood
Two years ago he made the ultimate sacrifice…he faked his own death to protect his wife from the terrorist he hunted. But now she is being targeted again, and the former air force officer will need to return from the dead to protect the woman he loves.

#1169 MAGNUM FORCE MAN by Amanda Stevens
Maximum Men
In all his years training at the Facility, there was only one woman who could draw him away—and she's in danger. Now he'll put all his abilities to work to save her.

#1170 TRUSTING A STRANGER by Kerry Connor
The only way to save her life and escape her ex-husband's enemies was to marry the attractive yet coldhearted American attorney. Neither expected their feelings would grow or that danger would follow her to her new home….

#1171 BODYGUARD UNDER THE MISTLETOE
by Cassie Miles
Christmas at the Carlisles
Kidnappers used her ranch as a base of operations, and now she and her little girl are their target. But first they'll have to get past her self-appointed bodyguard—a man who won't rest until she's safe…and in his arms.

#1172 OPERATION XOXO by Elle James
Just when she thought she had outrun her past, the first threatening note arrived—then there was a murder. The FBI agent sent to protect her is as charming as he is lethal, but can she trust him enough to let down her own guard?